Last of the Albatwitches

Brian Keene

deadite
press

DEADITE PRESS
205 NE BRYANT
PORTLAND, OR 97211
www.DEADITEPRESS.com

AN ERASERHEAD PRESS COMPANY
www.ERASERHEADPRESS.com

ISBN: 978-1-62105-159-6

Acknowledgements

My sincere thanks and appreciation go to everyone at Deadite Press, Jeff Burk, Carlton Mellick, Rose O'Keefe, Tod Clark, Mark Sylva, Stephen McDornell, Paul Goblirsch, Glenn Chadbourne, M. Wayne Willer, Alan M. Clark, Mark Umphrey, Johnny Thunder, Ken Kleppinger, Mary SanGiovanni, and, as always, my sons.

DEADITE PRESS BOOKS BY BRIAN KEENE

Urban Gothic
Jack's Magic Beans
Take the Long Way Home
Darkness on the Edge of Town
Tequila's Sunrise
Dead Sea
Entombed
Kill Whitey
Castaways
Ghoul
The Cage
Dark Hollow
Ghost Walk
A Gathering of Crows
The Last of the Albatwitches
An Occurrence in Crazy Bear Valley
Earthworm Gods
Earthworm Gods II: Deluge
Earthworm Gods: Selected Scenes from the End of the World
The Rising
City of the Dead
The Rising: Selected Scenes from the End of the World
Clickers II (with J. F. Gonzalez)
Clickers III (with J. F. Gonzalez)
Clickers vs. Zombies (with J. F. Gonzalez)
Sixty-Five Stirrup Iron Road (with Edward Lee, Jack Ketchum, Bryan Smith, J.F. Gonzalez, Wrath James White, Ryan Harding, Nate Southard, and Shane McKenzie)

The first half of this book—The Witching Tree—is dedicated to my grandfather, Ward Crowley, who once told me the story of a man he saw hang when he was a child. That story directly influenced this story.

The second half of this book—Last of the Albatwitches—is dedicated to Bob Freeman, my favorite real-life occult detective.

PREFACE

This book, *Last of the Albatwitches*, is composed of two novellas—*The Witching Tree* and *Last of the Albatwitches*. Both were published separately as limited edition collectible hardcovers. They are now collected together in this new volume.

This book features recurring character Levi Stoltzfus, an ex-Amish occult detective. Although prior knowledge of the character or his history are not required to enjoy this book, those wishing to read his adventures in chronological order should do so as follows: *Dark Hollow* (which serves as a prequel), *Ghost Walk*, *A Gathering of Crows*, and now this book. The final two novels in the series—*Invisible Monsters* and *Bad Ground*—should be available in 2015 and 2017 (unless you are reading this in the future, in which case, they are already available).

For the completists and collectors among you, Levi also appears in a short story titled "House Call" (which is reprinted in my collection *All Dark, All the Time*). That story takes place sometime between the events of *Dark Hollow* and *Ghost Walk*. Finally, an alternate reality version of Levi appears in the novel *Clickers vs. Zombies* (which was co-written with J.F. Gonzalez).

It should also be noted that this book also features characters and situations from my novel *Castaways*, and (to a much lesser extent) *Scratch* and *An Occurrence in Crazy Bear Valley*. Once again, knowledge of the events in those books is not required to enjoy this one. I offer the information only for those who are curious about my overall mythology and how the books tie together.

As always, I appreciate your support. Thanks for buying this book. You keep reading them, and I'll keep writing them.

Brian Keene

Somewhere in the backwoods of Pennsylvania
May 2014

PART ONE

THE
WITCHING
TREE

ONE

Ryan Laughman wasn't scared until he heard his dog, Dobby, give a pained and frightened yelp. Dobby was a Beagle. Ryan had named the dog after his favorite character in the Harry Potter series—the house-elf who had served the Malfoy family. Dobby was eight years old and a little fatter and slower than he used to be. Despite that, he was still able to do what his breed of dog did best, which was chase rabbits. If there were no rabbits available to chase, a groundhog would do, or a pheasant, or maybe a squirrel. One time, he'd even chased a fox. But for the most part, Dobby preferred rabbits.

Just like he always did, Ryan had let Dobby out when he got home from school. The Laughman's lived on a rural three-acre lot along Old Hanover Road, and their property was bordered with miles of farmland and forest. Dobby stayed cooped up in the house all day while Ryan was at school and his parents were at work. The dog usually stayed outside for an hour or so, coming back home when he heard Ryan's mother's car pull into the driveway, which indicated that the family—and Dobby—would soon be fed. Occasionally though, Dobby would catch the scent of a rabbit or a groundhog, and when that happened, all bets were off as to when he would return to the house. On a few rare occasions he'd stayed out all night, slinking home in the morning with his tail between his legs and his fur full of burs and seed pods, his tongue lolling from happy exhaustion.

Dobby was baying when Ryan's mother, Cathy, arrived home. She got out of the car, shoulders sagging, dirty-blonde

11

bangs hanging over her eyes—clearly exhausted from her shift as a waitress at the Cracker Barrel out on Interstate 83 near the Shrewsbury exit.

"Hi, honey," she said to Ryan.

"Hi, Mom." Ryan sat on the swing-set his parents had put up for him years ago. At twelve, he thought himself too old to use the seesaw or sliding board anymore, but he often sat on the swing. The dirt beneath his feet had a deep indentation that his feet had made over the years. He scuffed his shoes in the dirt. Dobby howled again. The sound echoed over the fields. The dog sounded very far away.

"Dobby found a rabbit?" Cathy Laughman asked.

"Yeah." Ryan nodded. "Sounds like it. Or a groundhog, maybe. Can I get Dad's 4-10 and go shoot it?"

"You know better than that." Cathy fumbled at the screen door, juggling her purse and her keys. "Your father said you can't use the guns without him around. Not until you take a hunter's safety course, and you have to be fourteen to register for those."

"But I'll be careful. Dad's let me shoot before."

"No, Ryan. You know the rules. Take your BB gun. You begged and begged for that thing, and now that you have it, you never use it."

"It's not powerful enough. If Dobby has a groundhog, BBs aren't going to do anything to it. They just bounce off."

"Well, that's probably for the best. It's not hunting season, anyway."

"You don't need a season to kill a groundhog."

"Still… no."

"Please, Mom?"

"I said no, Ryan. No means no. I shouldn't have to keep saying it. Take your BB gun or wait until your father gets home."

Sometimes, Ryan did just that. Dobby would corner his prey, and Ryan and his father, Jack, would track him after Jack got home from work. If it was a rabbit the dog had cornered, Jack would usually shoot it, hunting season or no. But Jack Laughman was working overtime at the Glatco paper mill this week, and he wouldn't be home until well after dark. He'd be in no mood to look for the dog. He'd barely be in the mood to do anything, other than have a few beers and watch whatever was on TV.

Dobby howled again, long and mournful.

"Please, Mom? Please?"

"You heard me. Now come on, honey. Don't argue with me. It's been a long and crappy day, and I'm tired."

Cathy went inside. Sighing, Ryan followed her. He went to his room and rummaged through the closet until he'd found his BB gun. His mother had been right. He hadn't used it since last year, just a few weeks after receiving it for his birthday, and he had to move clothes and boxes and other toys out of the way just to get to it. He searched some more until he found a half-full canister of BBs. Then he carried both the container and the rifle into the kitchen. His mother was peering into the cabinets above the oven, frowning.

"Your father's still on overtime. I'm not going to cook since it's just you and me tonight," she said without turning around. "You okay with Hot Pockets for dinner?"

"Sure. Pepperoni?"

"Absolutely."

"Can we wait till later, though?"

"Of course." She turned around and saw the BB gun in his hand. "Are you going after Dobby?"

Ryan nodded.

"Well, be careful. And be home by dark."

"Okay."

13

"I love you, baby."

"Love you too, Mom."

Without another word, Ryan had gone off in search of his dog. By his estimation, he had an hour or so until sundown. That was plenty of time to find Dobby and see what the old Beagle had cornered. What he hadn't counted on, however, was that Dobby had gone much further than he normally did. Ryan followed the persistent baying, smiling the whole time. Dobby certainly sounded excited. He crossed their property and walked across the cornfield behind their house. Then he made his way through a soybean field and a small thicket of woods. Dobby's barks grew louder. Shaking his head, Ryan emerged from the woods and into another field. In previous years, Mr. Harrison, who owned the nearby farm, had planted pumpkins in this field. But Mr. Harrison had passed away two years ago and his family had been trying to sell the farm ever since. A real estate developer was considering purchasing the land now. Ryan's parents had told him that the developer was planning on building a housing development. Neither of them seemed pleased by the prospect, but Ryan had been sort of excited by it. New houses meant the possibility of new kids moving into the neighborhood, and while he had plenty of friends at school, not many kids his age lived on this part of Old Hanover Road. The only one was Huey Crist, a fat kid who liked to eat paste in art class and wore really thick glasses whose lenses were always smeared with smudgy fingerprints. Ryan didn't bully Huey like many other kids did, but he didn't particularly want to hang out with him after school either, and so, with the exception of Dobby, his evenings and weekends were pretty lonely.

Dobby barked again, and Ryan's smile grew bigger. He spotted the Beagle far out in the middle of the field, dashing toward a tall, old tree. A rabbit ran ahead of him, darting back and forth. Dobby howled with excitement as he closed the distance. The tree seemed to tower over him and the rabbit both as they slipped into the shadows beneath its branches. As he started toward the dog and the rabbit, Ryan wondered for a moment why the tree was there. It was the only one in the entire field.

Then Dobby yelped, and Ryan's smile vanished. He ran across the field, his sneakers pounding against the hard-packed soil. Weeds brushed against his legs. Dobby lay beneath the tree, whimpering and panting. The rabbit had disappeared. As Ryan closed the distance between them, he saw a thick tree limb lying next to the dog. Dobby howled as he drew nearer, and Ryan noticed that something was wrong with the dog's hindquarters. His back legs and tail didn't seem to be working.

He knelt beside Dobby, sat his BB gun on the ground, and stretched out his hand. Panting harder, Dobby licked Ryan's fingers and whimpered again. Ryan noted a sense of urgency in the dog's tone. The Beagle tried to crawl closer, but couldn't. Ryan supposed that the tree limb must have fallen on Dobby. His heart pounded, and tears welled up in his eyes. His tongue felt thick in his mouth.

"It's okay," he whispered, petting the dog's fur. "It's okay, buddy. It's gonna be okay. Good dog. You're a very good dog."

Dobby licked Ryan's fingers again, and panted harder. Ryan tried tentatively to pick the wounded animal up, but Dobby growled. The dog's hackles went up and Ryan jerked his hands away.

"It's okay, Dobby. Good boy. I've got to get you home. Mom needs to take us to the vet."

Sniffling, Ryan wiped his nose with the back of his sleeve. He was just about to try again when something wet dripped onto his head. Another drop followed. Frowning, Ryan glanced up—and screamed. The rabbit dangled above him, impaled on a tree branch. Blood dripped from its fur. Ryan stared, mouth agape, as the branch shook. The rabbit's corpse flopped around on the end of it like a rag doll. Dobby growled again. This time, the Beagle sounded frightened. The branch shook harder. It occurred to Ryan that there was no wind.

He glanced back down at his dog, and there was a loud crack overhead. Ryan didn't even have time to look back up before a falling tree limb, much bigger than the one that had hit Dobby, crushed both him and his dog to the ground. Ryan coughed blood once. Twice.

And then the field was silent again.

* * *

"Ryan! Ryan, where are you? Answer me!"

"We should call the police, Jack."

Jack Laughman heard the tremor in his wife's voice. Cathy was close to panic. He tried his best to reassure her.

"He's probably just out of earshot, honey. You know how he is. When he gets focused on something, he doesn't pay attention to anything else. Like those frigging video games. When he's on Xbox, you could set a nuclear bomb off next to him and he wouldn't notice."

"I don't think that's it," Cathy said. "I can feel it. I'm his mother. I'm telling you, Jack—something is wrong."

Deep down inside, Jack knew his wife was right. He felt it too—a deep sense of foreboding and dread. A hundred different scenarios went through his mind, each one more terrifying than the last. Ryan had fallen down a well. Ryan had broken his leg and was lying out in the woods somewhere.

Ryan had suffered some kind of seizure (even though their son had never shown any signs of such a thing before). Ryan had been abducted by some sick pervert and was trapped in the trunk of a car... or worse.

Thunder rumbled overhead, slow and distant.

His stomach roiled. Jack swallowed hard, unable to voice his fears to Cathy. He needed to be strong for her. Strong for them both. He looked at her and tried to smile, but it was obvious that she saw right through the ruse.

"Call the police," he said, his voice thick with emotion. "I'll go look for him. I've got my cell with me."

"Okay." She nodded. "Be careful, honey. I love you."

"Yeah. I love you, too."

Jack headed to the garage, grabbed a big flashlight that he normally used for spotting deer and other game at night, and then hurried across the yard. Behind him, he heard Cathy sobbing as she rushed inside to call the police.

"Ryan," he called again as he crossed into the fields. "Ryan, where are you? Answer me, god damn it! You're scaring your mother."

You're scaring me, too, Jack thought. *Please be okay...*

Thunder rumbled again, closer this time. The breeze picked up slightly. Jack tried not to think about his little boy caught out here in a storm.

"Ryan?"

No answer. Jack's heart sank even lower.

He trudged through woods and fields and thickets, crossed a thin stream, and continued on his way, looking for any sign of his son or their dog. He listened for them, as well, hoping at the very least to hear one of Dobby's "Oh boy, I got a rabbit" howls. Instead, all he heard were a few birds chirping and one lone squirrel, chattering at him in frustration over the fact that he was intruding into the rodent's territory. He shouted again, but his cries went unanswered. He tried calling for Dobby instead, but again, was met with only silence.

Jack's cell phone rang. He fished it out of his pocket and glanced at the display. It was Cathy calling.

"Hey," he answered, breathless. "Did you get a hold of the cops?"

"They're on the way. Did you find anything?"

"Not yet. Don't worry, hon. I'm sure he's okay. I can feel it. Just stay calm. I'm betting he and Dobby just went too far and lost track of time."

"You don't really believe that, Jack."

"Cathy…"

"The police suggested I call the neighbors and find out if any of them have seen him. I'm going to do that. Call me if you find him, okay?"

"I will. I promise."

"I love you, Jack,"

"I love you, too."

Like his son hours before him, it was the last thing Jack Laughman ever said to her. He ended the call, locked the cell phone, and slipped it back into his pocket. When he looked up again, he had emerged into another field. He raised the powerful flashlight and swept the beam back and forth. There was an old, gnarled tree in the center of the field, and two small, still bodies lay crumpled and torn beneath its branches.

"No! Oh no, oh please God, oh no, nonononononono…"

Jack ran across the field, screaming his son's name. He was so focused on Ryan's unmoving form that he never noticed the tree limb swinging toward him until it smacked him in the face. His nose exploded and his jaw snapped. The blow knocked Jack off his feet. The flashlight tumbled from his hands. Another limb swept down, hammering it to pieces and plunging the field into darkness. Spitting teeth and blood, Jack managed to cry out once more before the thick, serpentine tree roots thrust their way up from the soil, coiled around his arms and legs and throat, and slowly strangled him to death.

The ground beneath him turned red.

* * *

Alan Clinton and Roger Morgan were the first officers from the North Codorus Township Regional Police to respond to the call. The force only had eight officers, and two of them were part-timers. Budget cuts, brought on by a steadily weakening economy, had brought them to this, and it was rumored that the township supervisors might lay two more officers off before the end of the next quarter. As a result, Clinton and Morgan were coming off the tail end of a ten hour shift. Neither man cared. Overtime was always welcome. Both men had mountains of debt. Morgan had a wife and two kids at home. Clinton had two ex-wives and three kids between them.

Clinton had always thought that these calls—any type of call involving a kid, in fact—were the worst. During his first year on the job, back when dinosaurs still roamed the Earth, one of his very first calls had been a traffic accident out on Route 116, between Spring Grove and Hanover. When he'd arrived on the scene, he saw a car that had slid off the road and hit a tree. The driver, who they determined later had been going way too fast given the wintry conditions, had slid off the road, head-on into the tree. The tree was undamaged. The front of the car was crumpled. So was the driver, who hadn't been wearing her seat belt and had flown right through the windshield. These days, an airbag would have prevented such a catastrophe, but it was the Eighties and not all cars had them then. Most of the driver's skin had been scraped off her face, and her head had split open on a rock. Worse than the driver, however, had been her three-year old daughter, who was trapped in the car—and still alive—when Clinton arrived. The girl died in Clinton's arms while they were waiting for an ambulance to arrive. He'd gone home that night and curled up on the floor next to his own three-year old daughter's bed, and cried softly. Two marriages and three children of his own later, that night still haunted him. He thought about it anytime they got a call involving a kid.

Situations like this were, in many ways, even worse than an injured or dead child. Missing children always conjured up immediate images of some sick fuck fresh out of NBC's *To Catch A Predator*, even if it turned out the kid had just run off to hide at a friend's house. While Morgan questioned the distraught mother, Clinton surveyed the house, noting everything with a calm, detached professionalism. The home was clean and well-kept. There were framed photos of the father, mother and missing boy on the mantle. Nothing seemed amiss at first glance. The wife showed no signs of physical abuse. Neither did the kid, at least in the pictures. Photographs could be deceiving, of course, but Clinton's gut instinct told him this wasn't a case of the boy running away or the parents having a hand in his disappearance.

He called in the State Police and the volunteer fire department for back-up, and searched the backyard and house while Morgan finished with the mother. Like the interior of the home, Clinton found nothing amiss outside. And there was no sign of the kid. He even ducked down and shined his flashlight beam inside the doghouse, making sure Ryan hadn't crawled inside of there. It was empty, except for a half-gnawed rawhide bone. Mrs. Laughman had told them that Ryan had gone to look for the dog. This seemed to verify that the dog was indeed missing, as well. Its chain lay in the grass, one end affixed to the doghouse, and the other end only a metal clasp that would have hooked onto a dog collar.

The volunteer fire department arrived just as Morgan finished up the initial questioning. Clinton and Morgan took command of the operation, and the search began in earnest. Clinton prayed to a God he no longer believed in that they'd find the kid alive.

As the darkness deepened over the fields and woods, it began to rain, a steady, sodden downpour that quickly drenched those outside.

"Great," Clinton groaned. "Just fucking great. Could it get any worse?"

* * *

Morgan reached the edge of the field, accompanied by a State Trooper named Ford and some volunteer firefighters that had split off from the rest of the search party. Clinton had remained back at the Laughman home, taking command of their efforts. Several officers were combing the neighborhood, interviewing people and looking for anything suspicious. The Fire Chief had remained behind, as well, ostensibly to help Clinton oversee things, although Morgan figured the guy was mainly just standing around bitching about billable hours and who was going to pay for the search. They all knew from experience that the bill would get tossed back and forth between the township and other involved parties, but ultimately, the taxpayers would shoulder the debt in the end. Unless, of course, this was a scam being committed by the Laughman family, like that

21

family in Denver a few years ago who had faked their kid hiding in a runaway hot air balloon just to get some media attention in their pitch for a reality television series. If that was the case, then the Laughman family would pay for the manpower and everything else involved in the search, along with a hefty court fine.

"This fucking weather," one of the volunteers grumbled. "Wish we would have dressed for this."

"Worry less about the rain and more about finding this kid," Ford, the State Trooper, told him. "If he's lost out here, how do you think he's enjoying it? Probably even less than you."

"Let's hold up for a second," Morgan said, pausing at the edge of the field. He peered into the darkness, but all he could see was a lone tree far out in the center of the field. Everything else was in shadow. The moon was completely concealed by clouds and the stars were nonexistent. The only sound was that of the falling rain. He reached for his radio and keyed the mic.

"Clinton?"

There was a pause, followed by a burst of static, and then Clinton's voice echoed in the wide open space.

"Yeah? Got an update for me, Morgan?"

"No, nothing yet."

"Nothing on this end either, or from the other searchers."

"How about the father? Have we heard from him?"

"Negative. Mother says he had his cell phone with him, but he's not answering. It goes straight to voice mail. Maybe he's out of range."

Or maybe, Morgan thought, *he did something to his kid, and he's getting rid of the body right now, and his wife is covering for him.*

Morgan hated thinking that way. He'd interviewed Cathy

Laughman himself, and she'd seemed genuine and sincere. She came off as a woman who was worried to death about her son's whereabouts. But even though he'd only been a cop for five years, Morgan had seen enough to know that everyone was potentially guilty until proven innocent.

He was about to respond to Clinton again when lightning flashed overhead, lighting up the field in an eerie blue-white glare. Ford grabbed Morgan's shoulder and gasped.

"Look there! The tree…"

The lightning faded, returning the field to darkness again.

"What was it?" Morgan asked.

"I saw something hanging from the tree," the State Trooper replied. "I'm sure of it. Could have been a dummy, like something kids would hang up during Halloween. But…"

Simultaneously, both officers shined their flashlights across the field. They let the beams trail over the tree. Sure enough, something was dangling from one of the upper limbs. It looked like a body.

"What the hell?" One of the firemen took a tentative step forward. "Shine your lights lower on the tree. I think there's more than one."

Morgan and Ford did as he'd asked. All of them gasped and grunted. There were three bodies hanging from the branches.

"Come on," Morgan said, beckoning.

He broke into a run. One by one, the other men followed him. The beams from their flashlights bobbed up and down in the dark. Mud sloshed beneath their feet and the rain beat down incessantly upon them. Morgan slowed as they approached the crime scene, for already, he knew that was indeed what it had become. Jack Laughman, his son Ryan, and the family dog were most certainly dead, judging by the condition of their bodies. All three had been impaled on the tree limbs. At first glance, given the amount of damage to their bodies, it looked like they'd been killed before being placed there.

"Oh fuck me," one of the volunteers whispered.

A second volunteer turned away, retching loudly and then vomiting all over his boots.

"Clinton," Morgan said into the radio. "Better send everybody to our location."

"Copy that. Did you find them?"

"Affirmative."

"Is it... bad?"

"Yeah... yeah, it is. I... I've never seen... this bad."

"We need to check their vitals," Ford said. "They could still be alive."

Morgan privately doubted it, but he kept the thought to himself.

"Be my guest," he said. "Although I don't know how the hell we're going to reach them. Whoever did this... they must have had a ladder or something. Right?"

"Either that," Ford replied, "or they were fifteen feet tall."

"Hey, guys?" Morgan turned to the volunteers. "Can you stay back a bit? This is a crime scene now. We need to proceed with an abundance of caution. Our primary concern is securing it."

They nodded in understanding, shivering in the rain. Morgan and Ford glanced at each other and then stepped forward. Morgan felt something hard beneath his heel. He looked down and saw a small, white stone sticking out of the mud. When he shined his flashlight at the ground, he noticed two more rocks, identical to the one he'd stepped on. They were spaced about six feet apart in a sort of semi-circle, and it appeared as if all of them had been buried beneath the soil until recently. Shrugging, he turned his attention back to the grisly scene.

"Look at this," Ford said, shining his flashlight around the base of the tree.

"Footprints?"

"No. The ground looks... weird. Like something was uprooted here. But all I see is the tree, and obviously, it's still standing. There's blood mixed in with the mud, too. The branches have kept the rain from washing it away. And it's far from the bodies. There's no way it just dribbled down from above."

"So they were killed over there and then placed—"

Morgan never finished, because at that moment, the tree moved and all he could do was scream.

TWO

Levi Stoltzfus was awakened by a knock at his front door. He was grateful for the interruption. He'd been dreaming of Rebecca again. It was the same dream he always had—Rebecca when they'd been younger, dancing through a cornfield, laughing as she playfully teased him. As always, he'd given chase, excited by the prospect of being with her in such a secluded spot where they were sure not to be discovered by the elders. And, as always, she managed to stay two steps ahead of him. Her laughter echoed. Birds chirped overhead. The sun beat down on them, warm and inviting.

And then the dream switched, because again, that was what always happened, both in real life and in the dream. He pushed his way through some upright cornstalks and there was Rebecca, laying on the ground, her eyes open but unseeing, her legs splayed, and her blond hair spilling out from beneath the askew mesh-knit bun on her head. Her dress was in shreds, and so was she. Her skin, formerly the color of cream, was now red, as was her tattered clothing and the ground around her. Then the corn rustled and he heard the demon laughing.

Yawning, Levi glanced at the digital clock on his nightstand and saw that it was twenty minutes until midnight. He'd only been asleep a few hours. He sat up in bed, stretching his arms and legs as the knock came again, louder this time. Had he not been sleeping, he would have been aware of the caller's presence before they'd even reached the door. Indeed, most people would have never made it that

26

far. A series of alert mechanisms in the form of mystical wards and circles of protection insured that. They formed an invisible barrier between the edge of the yard and his front door, each one stronger than the last. Only a few people were able to pass through them all unmolested, and without triggering an alarm. That meant the late-night visitor either had permission to pass—or that they were strong enough to break through. He doubted any nefarious intent, however, simply because his dog, Crowley, who was tethered in the backyard, would have barked at the first sense of trouble. Crowley's silence meant that he knew the caller, or that the caller meant no harm.

And even if Crowley was wrong, the invisible guardian lurking just inside Levi's foyer would swiftly and permanently deal with any intruder. That had only happened once in all the years Levi had rented this house. A warlock from the Kwan, upset that Levi had appropriated his *Book of Shadows*, had once made it past the wards and glyphs in the yard and through the front door. The guardian was there waiting for him, a coiled length of darkness hidden amongst the shadows where the wall met the ceiling. Levi hadn't been home at the time, but it had been easy for him to imagine what had happened next. The warlock had probably felt the guardian's presence a split second before he saw it, and then the invisible being had ripped him to shreds. Levi had returned home with nothing to do but clean up the still-wet evidence.

A third knock echoed through the house, and he decided that he'd better get up and answer the door before whoever was out there tried to come inside and the guardian did the same thing to them. He left the bedroom and walked down the hall, passing a painting a friend of his had given him, depicting the Colleges of the Magus—the Moon representing

27

thaumaturgy, the Sun representing alchemy, the Hand for necromancy, the Eye for divination, the Serpent for sorcery, and the Dagger for Hemomancy. The picture always made him smile, because it reminded him of his friend, gone six years now after an incident with a vampire in the sewers beneath Pittsburgh.

He passed through the next room—a combination den and library. All four walls had built in bookshelves spanning floor to ceiling. Two small armchairs, a love seat, coffee table and a small desk occupied the center of the room. A marble chess set sat atop the table. The pieces were crafted after various mythological deities. The shelves were loaded with old, unabridged esoteric and occult volumes— Frazer's *The Golden Bough,* the collected works of John Dee, Francis Barrett's *The Magus*, the *Book of Soyga*, the *Cipher Manuscripts* (including the Johannes Trithemius cipher), Guido von List's *Das Geheimnis der Runen*, Johann Scheible's *Das Kloster*, Cyril Scott's *The Initiate*, Parkes' *Fourth Book of Agrippa*, all of Aleister Crowley's occult work, Samael Aun Weor's *The Perfect Matrimony*, the *Theatrum Chemicum*, a translation of the *Alexandria Codex of Sofia*, and even a scattering of loose pages from the *Necronomicon*. The library filled Levi with a sad sense of nostalgia. Ever since he'd purchased an eBook reader, he hadn't spent much time in here. The device held digital copies of most of the volumes, and that was incredibly useful for when he was travelling, and for the simple economy of storage, but he missed coming in here during the evening on a cold winter night, and relaxing in one of the chairs, and perusing the books at his leisure. He missed the smell and texture, and the sounds the pages made. A digital device couldn't duplicate that. Nothing could.

The books weren't the only thing Levi had missed. He'd

missed this home, too. Granted, it was only a rental property, but he'd lived here for more than a decade now, and it was as much a part of him as Crowley, or his horse, Dee. When he'd first moved in, Levi had converted half of the two-car garage at the rear of the property into a stable for Dee. The other half had been converted into a woodshop. Levi spent most days making coat and spoon racks, furniture, plaques, lawn ornaments, and other knick-knacks. On Saturdays, he'd sell the items at the local antiques market. It was an honest, decent living, and paid for his rent, groceries, utilities, and food for Crowley and Dee. But Levi had another vocation, as well. Levi practiced a form of shamanism called Powwow, just as his father and his father before him had done. He cured people of their ailments using magic. His patients were mostly composed of the elderly (who remembered the old ways), the poor (who didn't have health insurance and couldn't afford to go to the hospital), and people who'd forsaken the mainstream medical establishment in search of a more holistic approach.

But powwow went beyond medicine. It was a magical discipline, just like any other, and sometimes, Levi was charged with doing more than helping the sick. Occasionally, his endeavors led him to be involved in other, more serious, occult matters. There were times when the Lord tasked him to be a protector. That had been the case recently.

Levi had left Pennsylvania four months ago, on his way to the Edgar Cayce Association for Research and Enlightenment headquarters in Virginia Beach to make a copy of their eighteenth century German edition of King Solomon's *Clavicula Salomonis* for his personal library. On the way there, he'd stopped for the night in the small town of Brinkley Springs, West Virginia and as a result, had become embroiled in a battle against five revenant servants of a powerful entity known as Meeble—one of a pantheon of similar entities known as the Thirteen. Levi had bested Meeble's servants by stranding the revenants on the planet Yuggoth, but he had picked up a supernatural infection as a result. The infection was a white, otherworldly fungus that would have eventually killed him, turning his physical form to liquid. Weeks of meditation, herbs and spells had finally cleansed all traces of the infection from his system. After that, he'd completed his delayed visit to the Edgar Cayce headquarters, and obtained a copy of the manuscript.

Then, before he could return home, Levi had taken a forced side-trip to Roanoke Island. That was where the revenants that had menaced Brinkley Springs had originally come from, and to insure that they could never return to Earth, Levi spent a week locating their mortal remains (buried for centuries and separate from their spirit forms, still stranded on Yuggoth). He'd taken great care to destroy every trace of their physical remains. After that had come the long journey home—just Levi, Dee and their buggy. He'd been back in Marietta now for a little less than a week, and still felt unsettled.

There was another knock at the door. Levi felt the guardian stir.

"Easy," he whispered. "I sense no malice. Down, boy."

The guardian relaxed. Another knock followed.

"Coming," Levi called. "Just a moment."

He whispered a simple, quick prayer as he reached for the doorknob. Then he turned it and opened the door. His closest neighbor, Sterling Myers, stood on the porch. Sterling often fed Crowley when Levi was traveling, and as a result, he was one of the few people who could pass through the wards of protection unmolested. Indeed, Sterling was completely unaware of the mechanisms.

"I'm sorry it's so late, Levi," he apologized. "Did I wake you?"

Levi smiled. "No worries, Sterling. I was merely resting. What's wrong?"

"There's… there's a cop over at my place. Plainclothes. I checked his identification. Detective from York County."

"He's a little out of his jurisdiction then, isn't he? Anyway, how can I help? Is he ill?"

"He is, but that ain't why I came to get you. Turns out this guy was asking for you by name."

Levi arched an eyebrow in surprise and stroked his beard thoughtfully. "Indeed?"

"Yeah. He wouldn't say what he wanted with you, even when I pressed him. See, I came outside to smoke, on account of the wife won't let me do it inside the house anymore. She says if I want to kill myself I shouldn't take her with me. Anyway, I'm outside smoking, and I see this car parked over there along the side of the road." Sterling pointed at a white four-door cruiser—standard unmarked police vehicle for Central Pennsylvania. "And there's this guy kneeling next to it, right there in the rain, throwing up in your yard. I figured maybe he was drunk or something. I could smell the puke from my porch. I seen that your lights weren't on, so I go over to the guy. Ask if I can help him. He says he's looking for you, but he got nauseous when he stepped in your yard. He tries again while I'm watching, and the same thing happens. He took a few steps onto your sidewalk and then bent over and threw up all over his shoes. Anyway, he flashed a badge then. Asked me to come get you. He's over at my house. I'm sorry about this, Levi, but he's a cop, you know? I didn't know what else to do."

"Well, I suppose we can assume that he's not here to buy furniture from me."

31

"No, I don't guess he is."

"Thanks, Sterling. Please tell him that I'll be right over. I just need to freshen up a bit."

"Okay, will do. Sorry again about this, Levi. Hate to drag you out in the rain and shit."

"It's okay. There's no need to apologize. You're a good neighbor and a good friend. I'll be right over. Just let me get something."

"Okay."

Sterling turned and headed back out into the rain, running across the yard. Levi went inside and returned to his bedroom, where he retrieved a slim, dog-eared, battered book from the nightstand. The dim bedroom light glinted off the tiny, faded gold lettering on the cover.

The Long Lost Friend
A Collection
of
Mysterious & Invaluable
Arts & Remedies
For
Man As Well As Animals
With Many Proofs

Of their virtue and efficacy in healing diseases and defeating spirits, the greater part of which was never published until they appeared in print for the first time in the U. S. in the year of our Lord 1820.

By
John George Hohman

I N R I

The book was a family heirloom. It had belonged to Levi's grandfather and then his father before being passed down to him. Levi never left home without it, not even for something as trivial as a walk across the street. Inscribed on the front page of the book was the following: *Whoever carries this book with him is safe from all his enemies, visible or invisible; and whoever has this book with him cannot die without the holy corpse of Jesus Christ, nor be drowned in any water, nor burn up in any fire, nor can any unjust sentence be passed upon him.* This was his primary weapon—an unabridged edition of powwow's main grimoire. Unlike the watered down public domain versions available online, this edition contained everything he needed to work his craft—unless, of course, the adversary he faced was immune to the ways of powwow. That had happened to Levi more than once during his career, which was why he versed himself in other magical disciplines, as well.

He put on a black cloth vest with many deep pockets. Like the book, the vest had seen a lot of obvious wear. It was also too snug around his middle these days, Levi noted. He slipped the book into the vest pocket located directly over his heart, and then retrieved his wide-brimmed straw hat from the coat rack by the door. He put on his black shoes. Then he went outside and crossed the street. Raindrops pattered against the brim of his hat. He passed by the unmarked cruiser. The engine ticked softly.

Sterling and another man stood on the Myers' front porch. The stranger appeared to be in his mid-thirties, and was clean cut, with sandy-colored hair and a well-trimmed goatee. He wore a tan raincoat and matching colored slacks. His complexion was pale, as if he was just getting over a virus. Levi stifled a smile, taking pleasure in the fact that his home's defenses did their jobs. Still, he sensed no ill intent from the new arrival. His aura was normal, and his demeanor and body-language didn't hint at malice or evil.

"Here he is," Sterling said to the visitor as Levi stepped up onto the porch.

The man stuck out his hand. "Mr. Levi Stoltzfus?"

"You may call me that." Levi shook his hand. The man's palm was wet and clammy.

"Detective Kraft, York County Regional Police. Thanks for meeting with me."

"It's my pleasure, Detective."

"Sorry for making you come out in this weather," Kraft said. "I was telling Mr. Myers, I got sick all of the sudden on my way to your door."

"I assure you, it's no problem, Detective. I'm sorry to hear you were ill. I trust you feel better now?"

"Yes. Mr. Myers' wife was kind enough to give me some ginger ale. That seems to have done the trick. Settled my stomach down a bit."

"Ginger does indeed have curative properties," Levi agreed. "Sadly, most ginger ale soft drinks don't actually have real ginger in them. I suspect the carbonation settled your stomach, though."

"Maybe."

"So," Levi said after a pause. "What can I do for you, Detective Kraft?"

"Well, frankly, sir, we need your help. Before I transferred to York, I used to be a cop in Hanover. I served with a Detective Hector Ramirez. We went through the academy together, in fact. Do you know him?"

Levi thought for a moment, and then slowly nodded. "I don't know him personally, but I'm familiar with his name. I believe a friend of mine once spoke with him on the phone, in fact. He was involved with the LeHorn's Hollow murder investigation a few years ago, was he not?"

"Yes, he was. He was the lead investigator that Spring, when all the murders were committed."

"And he retired soon after that. If I remember the media accounts correctly, he accompanied that novelist, Adam Senft, into the woods the night of the massacre."

"Mr. Stoltzfus, while I respect your Amish faith—"

Levi bristled at the comment. He hated it when someone automatically assumed that he was Amish, simply because he preferred the long beard and plain dress code of his former people, or because he still drove a buggy instead of a car. Yes, he had been Amish, but that was a very long time ago. He'd been cast out, and his excommunication had cost him everything—his family, friends, and community. Even his sense of self, for a brief period. He was no longer Amish. He owned a television and had a computer and used a cell phone. He took a deep breath, chiding himself for his pride. The detective had no way of knowing that, of course. Levi focused on him again, listening to what he was saying.

"I'm very sorry, Detective, but I didn't quite catch that. Would you mind repeating it?"

Kraft's tone grew terse. "I said I don't like playing games, Mr. Stoltzfus. I know for a fact that you were involved with Adam Senft. You were there the night of his death, after he escaped from the White Rose Mental Health facility. So there's no need to play dumb, or pretend that you only know about it through media accounts."

"Are you implying that I...?" Levi paused, unsure of how to proceed. He didn't want to implicate himself, since it was he, in fact, who had helped the novelist escape the facility in question—and further, had been directly responsible for the man's subsequent death.

"Calm down, Mr. Stoltzfus. I'm not here to arrest you

or implicate you in anything. I brought it up only because Detective Ramirez had some rather… unorthodox… beliefs right before he retired. Beliefs in the supernatural. Beliefs that I happen to share."

"I see."

"Do you?"

"I'm not sure I understand what it is you're getting at, Detective."

"Look, what I'm saying is that I'm familiar with your work. Your real work. Not the furniture-making or the healing. I know what you do, and I really need your help."

Levi glanced at Sterling and smiled. "Sterling, perhaps you could give us a moment alone?"

"Sure thing, Levi. Nice meeting you, Detective. Hope you feel better soon."

"Thanks for your assistance, Mr. Myers."

They waited until Sterling had gone inside and closed the door. Moments later, they heard the volume on the television get louder. Judging by the sound, Sterling was watching a replay of the Orioles game from earlier that evening, and the team was losing. This was confirmed when Sterling began cursing.

"What sort of problem are you experiencing, Detective?"

Levi listened while Kraft told him everything. When the Detective was finished, he nodded.

"Can you help me?" Kraft asked.

"Let me get my things from the house. You'll have to drive, if that's okay? All I have is my buggy."

"Of course."

While Kraft warmed up the car, Levi ducked into his home and gathered his things. He opened a brown leather kit bag and placed a number of items inside—red and white chalk, a metal compass, small bundles of dried sage and hemp, a pouch of crushed rose petals, a large canister of salt, vials of oil and holy water, a cigarette lighter, a knife, a silver ring, and a crucifix with a pewter figure of Jesus hanging from it. From his library, he selected a spiral-bound notebook in which he'd transcribed a number of various exorcism rituals, including those of the Roman Catholic Church, the Native Americans, some Essene translations, excerpts from *The Lesser Key of Solomon*, the Rabbi Yehuda Fetaya's *Minchat Yahuda*, the Throne Verse and the last three Surah from the *Quran*, portions of the Hindu *Atharva Veda*, along with the names of Narasimha, the Bhagavata Purana scripture, and the third, seventh and eight chapters of the *Bhagavad Gita*. Levi knew from personal experience that demonic possession and exorcism wasn't strictly a Christian problem, nor did it always require a Christian solution. There were many demons in the world—and beyond it. Better to be prepared for any eventuality. The notebook also contained key portions of Johann Weyer's *Pseudomonarchia Daemonum*, as well as a list of demons he'd printed off from Wikipedia. He intended to eventually transcribe the notebook onto his eBook reader, but hadn't yet had the time.

After placing the notebook into the leather bag, Levi patted his pocket, insuring that his copy of *The Long Lost Friend* was still there. Then he locked up the house and got into Kraft's car.

"Tell me everything," Levi said as they took the on ramp for Route 30. "I know you did already, but tell me again. Don't leave anything out, no matter how unimportant or trivial it may seem. The Devil is always in the details."

Kraft nodded. "Okay. But can I ask you what it is you think we're dealing with here?"

"That remains to be seen."

He glanced out the window, watching the Susquehanna

River rush by below as they crossed into York County. The windshield wipers and the rain both beat a steady rhythm. The radio was tuned to a classic rock station. Eric Clapton crooned "Bell Bottom Blues" softly in the background. Levi closed his eyes and listened while Detective Kraft told him everything again.

THREE

The exorcist wasn't what Clinton expected. It was after one o'clock in the morning when Detective Kraft returned with the "freelance troubleshooter" (as Kraft had described him before departing) and the Laughman family's driveway bustled with activity—local, regional and State law enforcement, the fire department, civilian volunteers, and the media. So far, Clinton had managed to keep the media and most of the civilians from learning the truth. As far as they knew, Ryan Laughman, his father, and the family dog were still missing, and search parties were looking for them. What he hadn't told them was that the three had been found, and they were dead, and that the perpetrator was apparently a tree, and that the tree had gone on to kill over a dozen men since then. As Morgan and Ford were slain, several volunteers ran forward to help them, while others radioed for assistance. Men converged on the scene in time for a slaughter.

Clinton watched as Kraft and the exorcist got out of the car and made their way toward him. The dark-haired newcomer was either Amish or Mennonite, judging by his manner of dress and his long, unruly beard. He appeared to be in his mid-thirties, but he carried himself as a man much older. While his complexion and build were still youthful, his eyes spoke of miles traveled. Officer Clinton wasn't sure what he had expected, but it certainly wasn't this. The man had a brown leather kit bag slung over one shoulder. It swayed and bumped against his hip as he stepped over puddles.

"Officer Clinton," Kraft said, "meet Levi Stoltzfus. Mr. Stoltzfus is here to help us with our… problem."

Clinton shook hands with the Amish man, glancing over at the media vans as he did so. A few of the more intrepid reporters were looking their way with clear interest.

"Maybe we should speak somewhere more private," Clinton whispered.

"There's no need," Levi said. "Detective Kraft fully appraised me of the situation on the journey here. I don't need anything else. At this point, the naming is important."

Both police officers nodded, pretending they understood what he meant.

"The site is secure?" Levi asked.

Clinton continued nodding. "Yeah. I've got a couple guys I trust standing guard at the edge of the field. Nobody is getting close to the crime scene. But I don't mind telling you, Mr. Stoltzfus, the guys are scared shitless. We all are. Pardon my French, but just what the fuck is happening out there? What is this?"

"That's what I intend to find out," Levi said. "Take me to the site. I would see this tree for myself."

* * *

They stood at the edge of the field—Levi, Clinton and Kraft, along with the few men who had been posted as guards. The rain had ceased and the clouds were beginning to slowly dissipate, revealing a bright and full moon. The tree cast its long shadow across the field. Bodies dangled from the limbs, and more corpses littered the ground around the base of the trunk. The wind blew, and the bodies hanging from the tree danced in an obscene pantomime.

"At least the damn weather cleared," Clinton said.

"How far does it extend?" Levi asked. "How close to the tree were the victims?"

"A couple of feet, maybe?" Kraft frowned. "Not too far beyond the limbs, at least."

"I'm going in. I need everyone else to stay here."

Kraft's frown deepened. "It's a crime scene, Mr. Stoltzfus. One of us needs to accompany you, at the very least. It's the law."

"It wasn't a request, Detective. Let me be very clear. You asked for my help because you've heard of my capabilities and because you think you have an inkling of what you're dealing with here. Well, trust me, gentlemen. You have no understanding of what we face. Neither do I… yet. That's one of the things I need to determine. And to do that, I need to go alone. I don't need an escort. What I need is to be able to do what I must to learn the identity of what this is. The longer we delay, the more dangerous this entity could become. Not to mention the harder it will be for you to keep this quiet. Right now, you've confined the situation to yourselves and a handful of others who've stayed quiet. That won't last much longer. When word gets out about what has happened here, you'll have the federal government, Black Lodge, and every two-bit would-be occultist and ghost hunter descending on this place. Believe me when I tell you that you don't want that. I promise not to disturb your crime scene anymore than is necessary. Agreed?"

"Fine with me," Clinton said. "I'm scared shitless just standing here. I don't need to get any closer to that fucking thing."

Sighing, Kraft nodded. "Okay."

"Thank you," Levi said, offering them a confident smile. Then he turned to face the tree, and bowed his head in prayer. The two officers glanced nervously at each other and then did the same. Levi prayed, "The cross of Christ be with me. The cross of Christ overcomes all water and every fire. The cross of Christ overcomes all weapons. The cross of Christ is a perfect sign and blessing to my soul. Now I pray that the holy corpse of Christ bless me against all evil things, words, and works. Amen."

"What happens now?" Kraft asked.

"Now," Levi replied, "I go see who or what we're dealing with."

"But don't you want a weapon or something?" Clinton ran a hand through his hair. "I don't know. A chainsaw, or maybe an axe?"

"No," Levi said. "I'll have no need of anything like that. At least, not yet."

"Well, then how the heck are you going to defend yourself? You see what it did to the others."

"Our adversary can't hurt me," Levi told them, "because I carry something on my person that prevents me from any harm it might attempt to do. I have something much better than the body armor your men wear."

"Oh yeah?" Kraft asked. "What's that?"

"A book… and my faith."

Without another word, Levi stepped into the field. After he'd only gone a few feet, the bottoms of his pants legs grew soaked and his shoes squelched in the mud. Levi kept his eyes on the vegetation around him, watching for unusual signs of movement. The weeds swayed in the breeze, but that was all. He glanced skyward and noted that there were no birds or owls or bats overhead. Neither was their any nocturnal activity in the field—no foxes or groundhogs. Granted, it could be all the human activity chasing them away, but Levi didn't think so. Animals were sensitive. So was he. And he could feel the entity's presence from here—a dark malignancy lingering over the field, coiled like a serpent beneath his very feet. The problem was—what *was* it? A demon, most likely, but from what pantheon?

Lord, he prayed silently, *here we are once again, You and I. And as always, I remain your humble servant and your mighty sword. I seek Your guidance and Your strength, Lord. I seek Your protection. Guide my hand in this endeavor as if it were your own. Let our victory be swift and just, and though my methods might not all be yours, let their purpose be to thy everlasting glory. On and in your name, Father. Amen.*

He drew closer. Levi wasn't afraid, but he was cautious. He'd dealt with more than his fair share of supernatural entities over the years. Indeed, almost three years ago, he had defeated Nodens, the most powerful member of the Thirteen, and stopped the beings' attempt to breach the walls of this Earth and drown it in eternal darkness, snuffing out all life. Their battle had taken place only a few miles from here, ending only when Levi offered up the local novelist Adam Senft as bait for a trap. Senft had died as a result. Levi had been afraid then. He wasn't now.

But in addition to being cautious, he was curious, as well. There were a number of possible deities he could be facing here, and he was still no closer to figuring out which one it was. In many ways, Levi mused, the same could be said for most of the rest of humanity. Every religious group—Christians, Muslims, Jews, Buddhists, Sikhs, Satanists, Pagans, Hindus, Scientologists and every other denomination, group or cult, no matter how big or how small—thought that their way was the right way. The only way. In reality, none of them knew the right way. They lived their lives and died without ever truly knowing or understanding the secrets of the universe. But he understood them. He understood them well. It was one of the reasons he had trouble sleeping at night.

It was one of the reasons he was alone.

He drew closer to the spot. Even without the malevolent presence inside of it, the lone tree was foreboding. It was a common enough sight in rural Pennsylvania. Farmers often left a tree in the middle of the field. Sometimes the trees helped with irrigation or offered shade for livestock or workers on hot summer days. Other times they were used to mark where rocks—too big to pull out and cart away—were buried, so that the plow blades didn't break on them. Sometimes the trees marked something else in the ground—an old foundation or a sinkhole or even a grave. He wondered if that could be the case now. Could there be a restless sprit buried beneath the tree, hungering for vengeance? A witching tree? It was a slight possibility, but Levi didn't think so. The presence hanging over the field was more potent than that. This was something more than a restless shade.

The suspicion was confirmed a moment later when he noticed the circle of white stones around the base of the trunk. Levi recognized them immediately. They were a circle of binding. More importantly, they were a powwow circle of binding. Whomever had erected them had practiced the same craft as him. That narrowed the possibilities to a more manageable level. An Arabic or Hindu demon wouldn't be effected by a powwow spell. Powwow worked best on Judeo-Christian deities. It was useful against other spirits from other cultures and religions, but not a definitive cure. It could even be used against one of the Thirteen, but only if the practitioner used it in conjunction with other methods and schools of magic. In this case, Levi saw no sign that such a thing had taken place. The stones looked old, and he surmised that the recent storm, combined with the roots moving beneath the tree, had pushed them up through the ground. They were still in place, which was good. Otherwise, the entity would have been loosed. He needed to exorcise and banish it before that happened.

Levi edged closer to the circle of stones. Then he raised his head and spoke aloud in a clear, strong voice, issuing a challenge of sorts— a passage from *The Long, Lost Friend.*

"Enoch and Elias, the two prophets, were never imprisoned, nor bound, nor beaten, and came out of their power. Thus, no one of my enemies must be able to injure or attack me in my body or my life, in the name of God the Father—"

The leaves on the tree rustled and the branches began to tremble. The bodies, dangling from the limbs like fruit, shook, arms and legs swinging wildly. It was just the reaction Levi had been expecting. It meant that whatever entity was residing within the tree was either Satanic in origin or had come from the Pit. Such beings reacted strongly or violently to such a challenge, as this one had just done. Levi decided to press on.

"Thus," he repeated, "no one of my enemies must be able to injure or attack me in my body or my life, in the name of God the Father, the Son, and the Holy Ghost. Ut nemo in sense tentat, descendere nemo. At precedenti spectatur mantica tergo."

The tree thrashed, rocking back and forth. The mud rippled as thick roots thrust themselves upward, grasping and wriggling. They slithered toward him, recoiling when they reached the limits of the stone circle.

"I, Levi Stoltzfus, son of Amos, command you to give me your name, unclean spirit. Whom am I addressing?"

The tree settled down again, the roots going limp, the branches growing still.

"I command you in the name of God to reveal your

identity. Give me your name!"

A large limb bent back like a catapult and flung a corpse out of the circle. Levi dodged to the side, and the mangled body landed in the mud. The victim's eyes had been gouged out. He heard a cracking sound, and at first, assumed it must have been the dead man's bones, but when the noise continued, Levi turned back to the tree. As he watched, writing appeared in the bark, as if carved by an invisible hand. The lettering was crude and the process was slow, but Levi watched patiently.

FUCK YOUR GOD

"Your name, spirit! It is not me who commands you, but God almighty, maker of Heaven and Earth. It is His son, Jesus Christ, our savior and Lord, who will return one day to judge the living and the dead."

Again, Levi waited while the entity responded. This time, the reply was a riddle.

HE WILL NOT RETURN, FOOL. HE CANNOT.
HE IS TRAPPED IN A LOOP.
DOOMED TO THE SAME FATE OVER AND OVER AND OVER AGAIN.

"Lies," Levi said. "But then again, your master is the Father of Lies, is he not? Now, again... what is your name? I demand that you reveal yourself to me."

This time there was no response. The tree stopped moving. Levi sighed.

"Fine. I guess we'll do this the hard way, then. Just remember, I gave you a chance."

Levi opened his kit bag, pulled out the canister of salt,

and walked the perimeter around the tree, pouring it out in a circle in an effort to reinforce the old stone circle of binding. When he was finished, Levi made the sign of the cross four times, to the north, south, east and west. Then he knelt down and let his left index finger hover over the salt, being very careful to avoid actually touching it.

"Dullix, ix, ux." He stood up and wiped his hands on his vest. "Don't go anywhere. I'll be back in a bit."

* * *

Clinton and Kraft were waiting for him when he returned. Both men's expressions were ashen. They rushed to his side.

"Is it over?" Kraft demanded. "Did you take care of it?"

"What the hell was it?" Clinton asked.

Levi calmly brushed their hands away and wiped the sweat from his forehead. "No, I'm afraid we've only just started. Detective Kraft, I'll need you to drive me again, if you don't mind."

"Okay. Where are we going?"

"To the library."

FOUR

"The…?" Kraft scowled in confusion as he followed Levi back to the car. "But it's three o'clock in the morning, Mr. Stoltzfus. The closest public library is the one in Spring Grove, but they aren't open this time of night."

Levi pulled out his cell phone, held up a finger to silence the Detective's protests, and then dialed. He paused for a moment, waiting, and then spoke.

"Maria? Hello! Yes, it's Levi. Yes, it has indeed been a long time."

Another pause.

"Well, how about now? You see, that's why I'm calling. I need immediate access to the archives. Can you get me in?" He looked up at Kraft and smiled, then said into the phone, "Great. I'll see you there. Oh, and I'll be bringing an associate with me. Is that okay?"

A third pause.

"And I can't tell you how much I appreciate it, Maria. You are a good friend." He snapped the phone shut and returned it to his pocket. Then he turned to Detective Kraft. "We're not going to the public library."

"Well, then where *are* we going?" Kraft asked.

"We're going to the newspaper's library. And they'll open for me."

"The newspaper? In York City?"

"Indeed. That is where the real magic happens."

"No offense, Mr. Stoltzfus—"

"Please, call me Levi."

48

"Okay, Levi. Don't take this the wrong way, but I don't see how going to the newspaper is going to help us. Can't you just, I don't know... make the sign of the cross and sprinkle some holy water on it?"

"If this were a movie, yes I could. But this is not a movie. It's real life, and in real life, it is knowledge that overcomes our foe and allows us to triumph. Knowledge is a weapon. We need the demon's name. Without that, I can't do much. We need information, Detective. The newspaper's archives are vast. They go all the way back to when York was the first Capitol of the United States. Indeed, they have information from even before that—personal accounts, documents from the County Historical Society, and similar things. Whatever is inside of that tree has been there for a very long time. That it has managed to go undisturbed this long is a miracle. There was a binding ring around it, and I suppose the stones might have prevented the landowners from plowing too close to the tree itself, but I find it hard to believe that no one has stumbled across its path until now. We need to retrace the history of the field, and see what we can find out. Then we will have our weapon."

Kraft nodded slowly. Levi grinned.

"I'm sorry, Detective. I suspect a lot of that didn't make sense to you."

"No more than a tree coming to life and killing people does."

"It's not the tree that worries me. It's what's *inside* of the tree."

"And that's a demon?"

"I strongly suspect so, yes. As I said, we just need to determine which demon it is."

"You suspect?" Kraft asked as they climbed into the car. "You mean it could be something else?"

49

"There's always a possibility. It could be a nature spirit. A dryad or nymph or perhaps something from the Native American canon. This area was, after all, once the seat of the Susquehanna Indian Empire. Or it could be something else entirely."

Kraft pulled out of the Laughman's driveway, weaving the car around the armada of fire trucks, police cars, ambulances and media vans.

"Like what?" he asked.

"Well, for example, there is a race of supernatural entities known as the Elilum. They are an incorporeal race, led by a deity known as Ab, who is a member of a group known as The Thirteen. The Elilum have the ability to possess the dead bodies of minor warm and cold-blooded life forms, as well as plant life after their soul has departed, in effect, turning them into zombies."

"Zombie... trees?"

"Indeed. As well as zombie insects, grass, and the like."

"That's ridiculous."

Levi arched an eyebrow. "I thought you said you believed in the supernatural, Detective?"

"I do. I mean, I think I saw a UFO once, when I was a kid. And I've seen other things, too. I believe it's silly to think we know everything about how the universe works. Telepathy, telekinesis—why shouldn't those things exist? But zombies? That's a little far-fetched. And zombie trees or bugs? That's nuts."

"There are some who say Jesus was a zombie."

Kraft squirmed in his seat. "I've got to tell you, Levi... you're the strangest religious man I've ever met. I'm a Methodist. I damn sure don't think my preacher would ever say something like that. "

Levi smiled. "There are zombies in the Bible, Detective,

along with sea monsters and UFOs and demons and all kinds of other things. And so are the Elilum. Ab is mentioned twice in the Old Testament, once in the Koran, and is also referenced in other texts of that era. The Elilum and their brothers were cast into a place known as the Void, and supposedly were unable to menace humanity once confined there, but there is reason to believe they might have escaped. Do you remember the forest fire that took place in LeHorn's Hollow back in the late Nineties?"

"Sure. A group of hunters died. They got caught up in it and couldn't escape, if I remember correctly."

"You are correct. There has been speculation that the hollow's original owner, Nelson LeHorn, may have somehow summoned a small group of Elilum, and that they subsequently possessed the trees there. The hunters may have encountered them, and in trying to fight back, may have inadvertently started the fire. Of course, there's no way to confirm that now."

Kraft was quiet for a moment. When he spoke again, his voice was lower.

"Ramirez told me that on the night of the second fire— the night of that massacre Adam Senft and his neighbors got caught up in—something was happening with the trees in the hollow. He never expanded upon it, but I got the impression that they may have somehow been involved in the death of one of our fellow officers at the time. But all of these things happened in LeHorn's Hollow, and that field behind the Laughman home isn't anywhere near there."

"Which is one of the reasons why I believe we're dealing with a common Judeo-Christian demon, rather than anything else. Hopefully, we can find something in the newspaper's archives that will confirm this."

They drove in silence after that. Kraft made a quick stop

at an all-night convenience store and bought himself a large coffee. Levi declined his offer to buy him one, as well.

"Technically, I should fast before attempting any exorcism," he explained. "That includes coffee."

"Should I fast, too?" Kraft asked.

Smiling, Levi shook his head. "There's no need. I'll be confronting the entity alone. Go ahead and drink your coffee. I believe you will need it, before we are done."

"That's for damn sure," Kraft muttered.

They drove through the city and arrived at the newspaper office. A few lights were on in the windows, but for the most part, the building was dark. The distribution center, located on the other side of the county, would be busy at this hour as the delivery carriers arrived to get their papers, but the office itself was nearly deserted, occupied by only a skeleton crew of editors and reporters. Kraft found a parking space and they approached the building. A strikingly beautiful, olive-skinned, dark-haired woman stood out front, smoking a cigarette. When she saw them, she stubbed the cigarette out on the sidewalk and smiled.

"Still a creature of the night, huh?" she said to Levi.

"Hello, Maria. Thanks again for meeting us at this hour."

"It's no problem. I figure I owe you. Who's your friend?"

"Detective Kraft, meet Maria Nasr."

"Hi, Detective."

Kraft shook her hand. "Nice to meet you. I enjoy your columns."

"Thanks," she said. "They're sort of tame, compared to Mike Argento's weekly rants, but I'm happy to let him take the heat from the public."

Maria let them into the building and led them through several low-lit rooms and cubicles until they reached a stairwell. She pushed open the door and motioned for them to follow her. The stairwell led to the basement. Maria flicked a light switch, revealing a large room with a state of the art climate control system and dozens of rows of alphabetized filing cabinets. Along one wall was a line of microfiche machines.

"Here you go," she said. "The filing cabinets have copies of every article we've printed in the last thirty-five years. Anything before that is on microfiche."

"It's not all on computers?" Kraft asked.

Maria shook her head. "The owner keeps saying he's going to digitize the entire library, making everything available on computer, but then he turns around and says we can't afford to do it. What are you looking for, exactly?"

Levi started to tell her, but Kraft cut him off.

"It involves an ongoing investigation," he said. "I'm afraid we can't discuss it."

"You mean the incident out in North Codorus? The missing kid and his father?"

"I really can't comment, Ms. Nasr."

"Anything you tell me is off the record," Maria said. "If Levi is involved, I can pretty much guess what's going on, and it's not the kind of thing we'd be able to print anyway. And besides, I've had the scanner on all night. The only other incidents are a shooting in downtown York and a car crash on Route 30 near Abbottstown. So, I'm guessing that I'm right. Call it journalistic instinct."

"I need everything on a particular property in North Codorus Township," Levi said. "And I do mean everything. Going back as far as you can. I'll also need files on the Township in general. I need to see if I can establish a pattern."

Maria whistled. "That might take a while. Do you know what you're looking for?"

"Not yet, but I will when I see it."

Maria spent several long minutes locating the files for him. There were a dozen thick, overstuffed folders full of articles. She also turned on one of the microfiche machines and showed Levi how to operate it. He experimented with the process, and then glanced up at them both.

"It's best if I do this alone, so that I can concentrate."

"Fine with me," Maria said. "That means I can go back to bed for a few hours."

"You're not driving back home, are you?" Levi asked. "Don't you have to be back in here in the morning?"

"We've got cots upstairs, for just such occasions. Won't be the first time I've slept here overnight. Come on, Detective. I'll show you where the coffee and stuff is in the break room. You can make yourself comfortable while you wait."

"Actually," Levi said. "If you don't mind, Detective Kraft, I'd like you to do something for me."

"Sure. What's that?"

"Do you have a way to access the courthouse files online?"

"No. And the courthouse is closed this time of night. Why? What did you need?"

"I was hoping you could look up the property deeds and such while I did this."

"I can do that without going through the courthouse. There are a number of websites that will let a person find that kind of stuff out. Especially if you happen to be in law enforcement."

"You can use my computer," Maria said. "Come on. I'll show you to my cubicle after we raid the break room together."

Nodding, Kraft followed Maria back up the stairwell. He glanced backward once and saw Levi sitting at a table with the file folders spread out before him. Then the door closed.

"So, how did you two meet?" he asked Maria as she led him to the break room.

"Remember the massacre at Ken Ripple's haunted attraction?"

"The Ghost Walk? I should. I was one of the detectives on the case."

"I thought I recognized you," Maria said. "I wrote it up."

"I remember. You used a really unflattering photo of me, too."

Maria grinned. "Sorry, Detective. Not my department. I'm only in charge of the words."

"That's okay. I've lost weight since then. Anyway, you were saying?"

"Well, if you're familiar with the case, then you know that Levi was involved."

"Somewhat," Kraft admitted. "I know he was involved, but I suspect the true extent of his involvement—and what actually transpired there—is still not known. To the general public, at least."

"You've got no idea, Detective. And I'll never tell. Suffice to say, we all owe that man a huge debt. I'm not sure what's going on right now, but whatever your problem is, Levi is a good person to have in your corner."

"I hope he can help."

"Not to be blunt, but if he can't, then you're probably fucked."

* * *

Levi quickly scanned the clippings, using a form of psychic divination that was part luck, part skill, and part intuition. He could safely disregard ninety-nine percent of what he read—accounts of township supervisor meetings, tax increases and engagement announcements had no bearing on the task at hand. He paid attention to the crime stories, however, as well as reports of missing persons, accidents, and oddities. When he found one that seemed to fit his still-developing pattern, he sat it aside and then returned to the pile.

After an hour, he placed the file folders in a neat stack at the edge of the desk and then flipped through the articles he'd sat aside. There were two missing person accounts. The first dated back to the Seventies—a local man who had vanished in the township while small game hunting. The second was from the Eighties, and involved a missing migrant worker. From what Levi could determine, neither man had ever been found. It was possible they weren't connected to this case at all, but his instincts told him differently. Both men, the hunter and the migrant worker, would have had reason to be in that field. Both could have decided for whatever reason to approach the tree, be it in pursuit of game or just looking for a place to sit and rest for a moment. Had they done this, the demon would have killed them, venting its frustration at remaining trapped inside the tree. It could have possessed the men, of course, but as long as the circle of binding was in place, the men would not have been able to leave the confines either, as long as the demon was inside of them.

Finished with the clippings, Levi took a seat at the microfiche machines and began pouring through the older records. He found two more disappearances, one from the Sixties and another from the Forties, as well as a report of a cattle mutilation in the area of the tree. He kept reading and searching, fighting off fatigue and trying to remain focused. Another hour had passed before he finally came across the story that he'd been looking for. As he'd predicted to Maria and Kraft, he knew this was the source as soon as he came across it. The account was from 1909 and concerned the lynching of a forty-five year old man named Todd Graham, as told by a man named Chester Williams. The article appeared to be a transcript of an oral history from the County Historical Society. Levi read on with interest, his fatigue suddenly forgotten, his mind clear and sharp and focused.

Being an Account of the Witching Tree, and Todd Graham, the Man They Lynched in Codorus in October 1909

by Chester Williams
March 31, 1964

My memories of Todd Graham are all good ones, which might surprise you, given his later lot in life and the things they say he did. He was a kind man, always polite to the women folk, and friendly to us children and to dogs and other animals, as well. I was twelve years old when they hung him, but I knew him since I was six.

He'd showed up in town one day, looking for work, as many folks did back then. He went to work at the sawmill over in Porters Siding, and took a room at the Sechrist's boarding house (which is now apartments). Neither the job or the room was much, even by old-timey standards, but a man could survive off them.

He attended our church and he was always very polite and well-mannered during the service and after, during fellowship. I heard him pray there, and when he sang along with the hymns, his voice was always very loud and clear. I think that's what I remember about him the most. His voice. It was very distinct, and pleasant to listen to. Until the change come along. Then he had a different voice.

I remember one time some bullies were teasing me down near Glatfelter's pond when I'd gone there to fish. I had a bucket full of Sunnies and Blue Gills and was fixing to take them home so my Ma could cook them up for supper, and the bullies come out and dumped the fish back into the pond. Then they threw the bucket out there too, and I started to cry. About that time, Todd Graham come along with his fishing pole and chased them bullies off. Then he patted me on the head and told me it would be okay, and cast his line out until the hook snagged the bucket. We talked for a while and then he told me to run on home, and said I should stay in school and study and never get into whiskey or gambling, and I'd be better than them bullies, who would have a hard lot in life.

Levi scanned ahead, eyes darting back and forth as he sped through the sentences. The remembrance recounted how this kind, religious, hard-working man suddenly changed in the author's twelfth year, exhibiting a series of shocking behavior. Levi found one paragraph particularly telling.

I guess Todd Graham lost his religion after that, for he started raising a ruckus with some of the others from the saw mill who liked their booze a little too much, and he took to sleeping in alleys and barns and once or twice right there in the street. He seemed drunk all the time, even when folks swore they hadn't seen him drink a drop. He showed up at the dance at the fire hall one night in September and when he spoke, his voice wasn't the same I'd heard in church. It was rougher and louder. Sounded almost like a different person. He caused quite a fuss, dancing with women in front of their husbands, even after they'd declined, and getting into fights. At one point, his friend Frank Burton come over to tell him to leave, and Todd Graham told him that he wasn't Todd anymore, but a man named Abalam.

The name was vaguely familiar to Levi. Pausing, he pinched the bridge of his nose and rubbed his eyes. Then he got up and fetched his kit bag, rummaging through it until he found his notebook. He perused the pages, deciphering his own hurried scrawl, until he found the name. Abalam was a lesser demon, one of the two hundred servants of Paimon, one of the Kings of Hell.

"A legion of two hundred," Levi murmured. "One of the Legion. You were probably never even missed. But how did you end up in that tree?"

He continued reading, skipping around and skimming to the important parts.

...and Todd Graham come into town shooting that night. He had a revolver in each hand, and he was firing up into the air, and hollering in that weird voice of his, the voice he'd come to tell people was Abalam's. I believed it, too. Others said he was drunk again, but I have to wonder. I remember how that voice sounded. What you've got to understand is that back in those days, we didn't know about these folks with split personalities and such. When he got to acting this way and talking like that, a person could almost believe that he really had become someone else.

A bunch of the men come out into the street and told Todd to stop, but he turned the guns on them and shot them down in cold blood. Only two of them had rifles, and Todd shot them first. He would have kept going, too, but Renny Glatfelter snuck up behind him and knocked him out with a length of kindling wood, on account of Todd had to stop to reload. The Constable locked him up in the jailhouse and Reverend Polk and that Powwow Doctor they call Rehmeyer came to pray over him.

Levi knew of Rehmeyer. The man had been an associate of Levi's grandfather back in the Twenties. He'd practiced powwow in York County while Levi's grandfather had practiced across the Susquehanna River in Lancaster County.

...the posse had twenty, maybe thirty men in it, and some of them weren't much older than me. All of them had masks on their faces, but I recognized a few voices as I watched out my window. I won't say who they were, even though most of them what did it are dead now. They took him out of the jail, and I seen that the powwow man was with them, only he didn't have a mask on. He didn't seem happy about the turn of events, but he wasn't doing much to stop it, either.

They took Todd Graham out of town, and nobody dared to interfere. I found out later that they took him to Harrison's farm, and hung him on the tree out there in the middle of the cornfield. I don't know if Mr. Harrison was in on the posse, but I do know that his brother Clyde was one of the men that Todd Graham shot. Way I heard it, the powwow man had wanted to try for Todd, but the rest of the men wouldn't have any of that. They said faith healing wasn't what was needed. The powwow man, seeing that he was outnumbered, made them wait while he did some kind of last rites, and erected some sort of circle of stones, and bade the other men help him to bury them. Only then would he let them hang Todd Graham, and the ones who did the lynching had to stand outside the circle, which I imagine caused them a lot of extra work. And extra rope, too. And that's how that old tree got the name of The Witching Tree, on account of in the years after, some folks said that Todd Graham was a witch or bewitched. Except that these days, most folks don't call the tree that anymore. Just us old-timers.

And there it was. The name of his adversary hadn't been found in his occult tomes at home, but here in the newspaper archives. It all made sense. Abalam had possessed this man, Todd Graham, compelling him to commit a number of violent acts and display increasingly uncharacteristic behaviors. The powwow practitioner, recognizing the situation for what it was, had wanted to perform an exorcism and send the demon back to Hell, but the townspeople had refused such a lengthy process. Desperate to stymie the demon, the warlock had done the only other thing possible, given the mob rules situation—he had quickly erected a circle of binding and trapped the demon inside of it. Upon Todd Graham's death, Abalam had been freed, but was unable to possess anyone else or escape back to Hell. Thus, the demon had been forced to possess the only other living thing inside the circle—the farmer's tree. And Abalam had been there ever since, trapped inside the tree and unable to leave. It seemed like a long time in human terms, but it was merely the blink of an eye for a demon. Still, Abalam's anger and indignation must have been powerful indeed, made worse by the fact that if another living creature stumbled into the circle, and the demon left the tree and possessed them instead, his situation wouldn't improve. Instead, Abalam had spent the convening years simply killing anything unlucky enough to stray within his reach.

Levi stood and stretched. His joints popped, sounding very loud in the silence. He gathered his notebook and kit bag, turned off the microfiche machine and the lights, and returned upstairs to find Kraft sequestered in Maria's cubicle. The Detective was speaking with someone on his cell phone. After eavesdropping for a moment, Levi determined that he was speaking with Clinton. Levi cleared his throat and Kraft glanced up.

"I've got to go. No, it's fine. Do the best you can. We'll be back soon." He put the cell phone in his pocket and stood up. "Find what you were looking for?"

"Oh, yes." Levi nodded. "Most definitely."

"I did, too. I checked on the property for you. It's been in the same family for three generations now. Folks by the name of—"

"Harrison," Levi interrupted.

"Yeah." Kraft sounded surprised. "How did you know that? Did you read my mind or something?"

"I told you, Detective," Levi stifled a grin. "Newspapers are magic. I got all of the information we needed downstairs."

"Did you also know that the landowner passed away two years ago, and the property failed to find a buyer during the estate sale, on account of the economy, of course? It's been sitting there unused."

"That would explain why the field hadn't been plowed recently," Levi said. "Well done, Detective Kraft."

"A developer is considering buying it though. Can you imagine what would happen if they sent bulldozers and contractors out into that field?"

"Then we must make sure that doesn't happen. Let's go."

"Should we thank Maria first?"

"There's no need to wake her up, and in truth, we've delayed long enough. Certainly longer than I like. The more we delay, the greater the chances that another of your officers or some well-meaning civilian will stumble into the demon's perimeter. I would be done with this."

"So what happens now?"

"Now?" Levi's grin grew broad. "Now, in the popular idiom of today's youth, we go bust a cap in the demon's ass."

Levi chuckled as they left the office building.

"Yeah," Kraft muttered. "Strangest damn religious man

I've ever met."

He didn't think that Levi had heard him, until the man suddenly stopped and turned around, fixing him with a glance.

"If you think I'm weird, Detective, you should really meet some of my associates."

The sun was just starting to rise over the city as they walked to the car. The air was already warm and inviting. Traffic was light and birds chirped overhead. It was going to be a beautiful day. Despite that, Kraft found himself shivering.

FIVE

By the time they arrived back at the Laughman house, dawn had turned into daylight, and the number of people lingering at the home had tripled. The media were demanding answers, and when Kraft and Levi found Clinton, the frazzled officer was clearly at wit's end.

"I was starting to think you two got lost," he grumbled. "What the hell took you so long?"

"We were preparing a battle plan," Levi told him. "Forewarned is forearmed. I had to make sure we were armed."

"Well, now that you're back, would one of you mind telling me how we're going to deal with this cluster-fuck? The Laughman woman is sedated, but I've got relatives demanding answers, and reporters out crawling around in the woods, and some more of volunteers who came across the crime scene. It's getting harder and harder to keep this quiet—and to be quite honest, I'm not sure we should be at this point. Maybe people need to know what's going on here."

"I would advise against making the particulars public," Levi said, "unless you want Black Lodge and other interested parties sweeping down on this place."

Clinton blinked. "Who? Black what? Is that supposed to mean something to me?"

Levi pushed past him and made his way through the crowd. Kraft whispered in Clinton's ear, urging him to hold it together just a little while longer, and then hurried after the magus.

"Are you ready?" he asked.

"I am." Levi nodded. "And again, I must ask that you stay out of the field. If Officer Clinton is correct, then it sounds like you'll have your hands full keeping people back, in any case."

"Yeah, it sounds that way. Do you have everything you need?"

"I do. I have my faith in God. As the Bible tells us, He helps those who help themselves." Levi held up the brown leather kit bag. "I've helped myself to everything in here. The Lord will do the rest."

They rushed back to the field. Kraft was dismayed to see that Clinton had been right. Several more people had converged on the scene. Luckily, the media wasn't among them—yet. But it was only a matter of time until one of the civilians posted it to Twitter or Facebook, or simply walked back to the command station and told others. He saw no one around the crime scene, and was grateful for that. At least his men had managed to keep that secure.

"Stay here," Levi warned him again. "And no matter what you see or hear, don't come out there. Okay?"

"Okay. Is there anything I can do to help?"

"Yes. Keep everyone back. And pray, if you are so inclined. Ask the Lord to lend me His strength and protection."

Then, without another word, Levi strode into the field, his head held high. He felt his pulse throbbing in his ears, and his skin felt flushed. He focused on his breathing, trying hard not to hyperventilate. While the exorcism itself was fairly uncomplicated, there were a number of variables that made him uneasy. He hadn't properly fasted, for one. Normally, he should have done so for three days prior to attempting this. And then there was the human factor. While he trusted Kraft not to rush forward, he was uneasy about all the other people converging on the site. If any one of them interfered or distracted him, even for a moment, it could change everything.

Levi opened the kit bag as he walked. He fumbled around inside of it until he found the silver ring he'd brought from the house. He slipped the ring onto the middle finger of his left hand. Then he spoke aloud, offering an invocation prayer.

"The blessing which came from heaven, from God the Father, when the true living Son was born, be with me at all times. The holy cross of God, on which He suffered His bitter torments, bless me today and forever. The three holy nails which were driven through the holy hands and feet of Jesus Christ, bless me today and forever. The spear by which His holy side was pierced and opened, protect me now, today and forever. May the blood of Christ and the Holy Spirit protect me from my enemies, and from everything which might be injurious to my body and my soul. Bless me, oh you five holy wounds in order that all my enemies may be driven before me and bound and banished. All those that hate you must be silent before me, and they may not inflict the least injury upon me, or my house, or my premises. And likewise, all those who intend attacking and wounding me either spiritually or physically shall be defenseless, weak, and conquered. The cross of Christ be with me. The cross of Christ overcomes all water and every fire. The cross of Christ overcomes all weapons. The cross of Christ is a perfect sign and blessing to my soul. Now I pray that the holy corpse of Christ bless me against all evil things, words, and works."

As he approached the tree, he clenched his fist, feeling the ring taught against his skin. "Guide my hand, Lord. Your will be done, as always."

He stopped at the edge of the salt circle he'd fashioned

earlier. The tree branches shivered in anticipation.

"I'm back," Levi said to the tree. "I told you I would be. Are you sure you don't want to come out now? I'm offering you one last chance to leave this place and go back to where you came from. All you have to do is ask for it, and I shall grant your plea."

The tree shook, limbs rustling and groaning. The corpses jiggled.

"Okay. Have it your way, then."

Sighing, Levi sat his bag on the ground. He knelt beside it and pulled out the metal compass, his knife, the small bundle of dried sage, the remainder of his salt, the vial of holy water, the cigarette lighter, and the crucifix with the pewter figure of Jesus hanging from it. After a moment's consideration, he returned the crucifix to the bag.

"And so... the hard way. You will not like it, demon."

Levi consulted with his compass. Then he picked up the salt and began to walk the perimeter, pouring it in a thin line to form a triangle on the outskirts of the circle. He did this by walking south, then east, and then upwards to form the triangle's point. The demon tried to distract him with more writing in the tree trunk, but Levi ignored the attempts. When he was finished, Levi gathered the dried sage and set it on fire with the lighter. Then he laid the smoldering clump down in the mud. He wasn't worried about the field catching fire. The weeds were still wet from the previous night's rain.

"So," Levi said, addressing the tree. "I've already given you my name, but what should I call you? You haven't given me yours, and it would be nice to know who I'm addressing. Should I call you Fred, perhaps? Or maybe Elias? No, those aren't very demon-like names, are they? And that's what you are, after all. You're a demon. One of Paimon's lot."

At the mention of its master's name, the tree grew still.

Levi could feel the fear in the air—an almost electric charge that made the hair on his arms and the back of his neck stand up.

"But which one? You're not Beleth. He is far too wise and cunning to ever end up in this trap you've found yourself in. Nor are you Calibrax or Nethal or Labal or Deluthar. There are so many of you making up the Legion. I could name the rest of your kind, but with two-hundred of you to choose from, we'd be here all day, and I am very tired. Therefore, why don't we just cut to the chase?"

The bark of the tree groaned and splintered as new words appeared in the wood.

YOU BLUFF. I WILL SPLIT YOU OPEN LIKE RIPE FRUIT.
MY ROOTS WILL DRINK YOUR BLOOD.

"You'll do nothing of the sort, and I'd like you to keep your roots to yourself, thanks very much. You know, it occurs to me how very frustrating this must be for you. It is written that you had a great speaking voice—a roar of sorts, rough and guttural. How disconcerting it must be for you to have to communicate by carving your letters into the bark of that tree like some lovesick teenager fashioning a heart and his girlfriend's initials."

YOU KNOW NOTHING, LITTLE MAGUS.

"Oh, but I do, Abalam. I do. Your name, for starters. And that's really all I need to know, isn't it?"

At the mention of the demon's true name, the tree shook so violently that it nearly surged out of the ground. The roots bulged and thrashed, thrusting up from the soil like live electrical cables. The branches shook, the leaves rustled, and the larger limbs groaned and thrashed. The bodies fell from the tree, landing unceremoniously in the mud. Nonplussed, Levi consulted his compass again and then stood facing to the northwest.

"I, Levi Stoltzfus, stand here today facing the house of Paimon. I wear a silver ring on the middle finger of my left hand in tribute to him, one of the Kings of Hell, servant of Lucifer, commander of they who are known as Legion, teacher of all arts, philosophy and science, knower of secrets, and keeper of the mysteries of earth, wind and water. I stand in the appropriate manner. I stand firm and resolute. I stand offering respect. Ut nemo in sense tentat, descendere nemo. At precedenti spectaur mantica tergo. Hecate. Hecate. Hecate."

As Levi chanted, the leaves of the tree began to change, turning from green to brown, and then transforming into serpents. Each of them was about twelve inches long, and the width of a middle finger. Hundreds of them appeared, wriggling from their places on the branches. Then, as one, they slipped to the ground and scurried toward him.

"They will do you no avail," Levi shouted, arms raised high. "For it is written that He laid hold of the dragon, that serpent of old, who is *the* Devil and Satan, and bound him for a thousand years! And He cast him into the bottomless pit, and shut him up, and set a seal on him, so that he should deceive the nations no more till the thousand years were finished."

The snakes slithered closer, edging up to the stone circle. Levi noticed that their eyes were pure black. He wasn't sure if they could breach the walls of the binding circle or not, but decided to take no chances. Thinking quickly, he switched to a passage from *The Long Lost Friend.*

"God has created all things, and they were good. Only you, serpent, are damned! Cursed be you and your sting. Get thee hence. Three false tongues have bound thee, three holy tongues have spoken for thee. The first is God, the Father. The second is God, the Son. The third is God, the Holy Ghost."

"I TOLD YOU BEFORE," the serpents hissed as one, in a great and terrible voice. Levi assumed that this was the same voice Todd Graham had spoken in when possessed by Abalam. It sounded like a lawnmower chewing up bits of glass in a tornado. "THERE IS NO HOLY GHOST. THE TRINITY IS MERELY TWO. THE THIRD IS LOST."

"You lie."

"I DO NOT. THE HOLY TRINITY IS ASUNDER. YOUR FAITH IS BUILT UPON A FALSEHOOD!"

For a brief moment, Levi felt a twinge of doubt. Could the demon be telling the truth?

"YOU KNOW IN YOUR HEART THAT I AM CORRECT. YOUR GOD HAS LIED TO YOU."

Levi raised his voice, shouting over the snakes. "Flesh and blood are born on thee, grown upon thee, and now lost from thee. I take them back in His name. Ito, ala Massa Dandi!"

Instantly, the snakes turned into salt. Their forms were solid for a brief moment. Then the wind picked up and they crumbled into piles. Grains of salt were scattered across the ground. Levi bent over, snatched the knife and straightened again. Before the demon could summon something else, he gritted his teeth and ran the blade across the palm of his right hand, slicing into the flesh. His stomach roiled from the pain, but Levi forced such considerations aside and focused on the task at hand. The ground trembled as the tree uprooted itself. Slowly, it lumbered toward him, the roots acting as tendrils.

"You cannot breach the circle," Levi said, flinging a fistful of his blood at the tree. It splattered across the bark. Tiny wisps of smoke rose from where the drops had landed. "You are scattered, Abalam. With the blood of the five holy wounds, I bind thee. In the name of the Father and the Son and the Holy Ghost, you are enchanted and bound. And now, I order you to leave this place."

Laboriously, the tree crept closer. The air was suddenly filled with the sound of trumpets and cymbals.

It's not working, Levi thought. *Why is it not working? I did everything correctly. My faith is strong. I invoked the Holy Trinity...*

The cacophony changed from musical instruments to the shriek of a crashing airplane. Despite the fact that he knew it was trickery, Levi glanced upward anyway. The sky was clear overhead—bright blue, with wispy clouds drifting by. It was an ironic contrast to what was transpiring below. He shook his head, focusing on the task.

"By His blood I bind thee. By His blood I command thee. By His blood, which was shed for me, do I trod on thee. I order you to leave this place!"

The tree stopped moving, but Levi could sense that the demon was still very much present. Steeling himself, he reluctantly called upon another power.

"I call upon Paimon to retrieve this wayward footman. I humbly ask that you return your servant Abalam to that which is Legion. I beseech you to hear my plea, and judge it to your liking. Appear to me, Paimon, that we may hold palaver!"

Holding his breath, Levi closed his eyes and bowed his head. He sensed, rather than saw, the field change around him. The breeze stopped, and time itself seemed to stand still. There were no insects or birds, no sounds from the men at the edge of the field. The weeds didn't rustle as he rocked backward on the balls of his feet. Neither did the few remaining leaves on the tree. And then, there was a voice.

"Look at me."

The voice was neither male nor female, young or old, powerful or weak, happy or angry. It simply *was*. Hesitantly, Levi did as commanded, opening his eyes and raising his head. Before him, seated atop a large black camel with red, bulging eyes, was a man with an effeminate face. He had an athletic build, like that of a weightlifter, but his hands, lips, eyes, and cheekbones were distinctly those of a woman. Atop the man's head was a golden crown encrusted with multi-colored jewels. Both the man and his mount were within the confines of the circle, standing next to the tree.

"Levi Stoltzfus," the demon said. "Long have my brothers and I wished to make your acquaintance. Your reputation precedes itself. Baal still rages over the insolence you showed him in Syria, and Nergal is consumed with shame over the defeat he suffered at your hands in Miami."

"Then Baal should have shown me the proper respect, and Nergal should have never infected that boy's preparatory school with his influence."

"Bold words, warlock. Can you back them up against one such as I?"

"Lord Paimon, I do not wish to fight with you. Indeed, I have summoned you with a humble heart, seeking only your assistance. I believe you know this to be true."

"This summoning was not proper. I see no sacrifice or offering. I should be insulted."

"I had no time to prepare a sacrifice, Great Paimon, for in truth, I had not planned on requiring your services."

"Your God has forsaken you, has He?"

Levi bit his bottom lip and said nothing. The demon

laughed. The Hell-camel snorted sulfur fumes from its flaring nostrils.

"My dear minion told you before. Things are not as you think they are in Heaven. The Trinity is asunder, and has been for some time. The Labyrinth falls into disarray and the walls of reality grow thin. The end of times is almost upon us. Soon shall come the war between The Thirteen and the Creator, and our forces will be there to seize control when both sides have defeated each other. Whatever it is that you intend here is pointless."

"I ask a boon, Paimon. Only that and nothing more."

"A boon? I see no offering. This is unacceptable, no matter what your intentions were."

"I have an offering. I can offer my services!" Even as the words tumbled from his mouth, Levi regretted them.

The demon's eyes narrowed. "Your services? And what makes you think I'd have use for your services, Levi Stoltzfus?"

"If you know my name, then that's answer enough, Paimon. You know what I am capable of. Render to me this boon and I shall return the favor in kind."

The demon frowned, stroking its chin as it considered the offer. Levi waited, trying hard to conceal his fear.

"It would have to be at a time of my choosing. You shall not know the hour, nor the task, until it is at hand. Do you these terms acceptable and fair enough?"

Shuddering, Levi let out a deep breath. "I agree to those terms."

"Then speak your mind, magus. What is it you ask of me? What boon shall I grant? Do you wish to know secrets? Do you desire a familiar? Shall I bind someone to your will?"

"None of these, lord. I ask only that you collect your servant, the demon known as Abalam, one of the many who are Legion, to your command in Hell. I ask that he bother the people of this planet no more. I ask that this ground be cleansed of his presence. Only this and nothing more."

"Very well."

And just like that, it was over. There was no cinematic flash. No burst of thunder overhead or a cloud of mist seeping up from the ground. One moment Paimon and his demonic mount stood beside the tree, and in the next instant, they were gone. So too was Abalam. Levi could sense the demon's departure. Seconds later, his senses were confirmed as the old tree began to splinter and crack. He scrambled out of the way just in time as it tottered forward and then crashed to the ground, breaking the circle of binding.

"The power and the glory forever," Levi whispered. "Amen."

But for the first time in his life, Levi did not feel the strength of those convictions. Instead, he felt unsettled and afraid, as if part of his soul had left him.

He gathered his belongings, returned them to the kit bag, and then wearily made his way back across the field. As he walked, he puzzled over the demon's riddle. What had they meant about the Holy Trinity being asunder? And why had God deserted him during the exorcism? Why, when he had called upon the power of the Holy Spirit, had he felt no response? And what of Paimon's warning about the end of times? Levi's mind reeled. What did it all mean for him, and more importantly, for the world?

"Are you there, God?" he whispered. "It's me, Levi."

The only response was the breeze, ruffling his hair.

Levi reached the edge of the field to find that Kraft was there, waiting for him. The detective's eyes were wide and bloodshot.

"Are you okay?" he asked.

Levi nodded. "I am. Thank you for your concern."

"What happened out there?"

"I won."

"Yeah, but how?"

"What did you see?" Levi asked.

"Not much," Kraft admitted. "It was weird. We saw you doing... whatever it was that you were doing. The exorcism, I guess. But then things got blurry, as if we were watching you through a distorted camera lens. Does that make sense? It was like when you're driving on a hot summer day and you see those waves of heat rising up from the road. That's what it looked like was surrounding you. Everything was blurry. At one point, I thought I saw someone there with you, but I wasn't sure."

"There was someone," Levi said. "But be thankful you couldn't see them. I only wish that I could say the same."

"What do you mean?"

Levi shook his head. "Nothing. It's not important. Only that I'll see them again at some point down the road, and I'm not looking forward to the reunion."

PART TWO

LAST OF THE ALBATWITCHES

ONE

April ran as if Satan himself was hot on her heels, and given her panicked state, the thing chasing her through the woods could have been just that—the Devil. Branches whipped at her face, raising welts as she fled. She tripped over a rock, tumbled to the forest floor, and then sprang to her feet again, oblivious to the cuts and scrapes, and the blood trickling down her forearm. She paused for a moment, gasping, but then a monstrous cry echoed seemingly from all around her, and she ran again. Thorns tugged at her hair and the tattered remnants of her clothes. She barely felt them. Indeed, April was operating more on instinct than anything else. Her only thought was to escape and survive. But then, as the howls and grunts of her captor slowly faded, April began to reason again.

She hunkered down in the middle of a thick clump of underbrush, realizing too late that there was poison ivy mixed in among the foliage. The waxen leaves glinted in the light of the almost-full moon. April didn't care. She'd gladly suffer poison ivy all over her body if it meant she'd make it out of the woods alive. She finally noticed the thin line of blood trickling down her wrist and forearm, and the other cuts and scrapes that dotted her palms and legs. None of them looked especially deep or dire. She'd worry about them when—if—she got home.

Biting her lip, she fought to control both her breathing and her fear. She was shaking so badly, April was sure the movement would give away her hiding spot. Bile rose in her throat, and she grimaced, tasting tequila.

Shock, she thought. *I'm in shock. Or else still drunk. Or both ...*

Yes, April decided. It was probably both. And if she made it out of here alive, the first thing she was going to do was find Tom and beat the living shit out of him. This was all his fault, after all.

Clear-headed but still fearful, she remained where she was, crouched in the undergrowth, bleeding, quaking, and listening for her pursuer. To make matters worse, she had to pee. She idly thought back to when she was a child, and summer afternoon games of hide and seek. She'd always had to pee then, as well. What was it about hiding that invoked the need to piss?

The forest was quiet. Not only did she not hear the creature, but there were no other sounds, either. No birds or insects or animals seemed present. In April's mind, that just made things worse. She was by no means a farm girl, but she knew enough about the woods to know that when the forest was this silent, it meant a predator was on the prowl. If only she had remembered that earlier, the first time everything had grown quiet.

While she waited for her trembling to subside, April tried to focus. She needed to find the road, or at least one of the hiking trails, but she had no idea where either of them were. She tried to retrace her steps in her mind, but her memories of the evening were hazy.

She'd been drinking at the Burning Bridge bar in Wrightsville with her boyfriend, Tom, and some of their friends. It had not gone well. It never did when Tom was drinking. He didn't get silly, like her friend Tammy's boyfriend did. Nor was Tom a violent or belligerent drunk. Instead, he became depressed. The more intoxicated he got, the more that depression deepened. Six beers and a few shots of tequila could put him in the blackest of moods.

April couldn't remember what had started their fight. There was no one thing she could put her finger on. Instead, as best she could recall, it had been a series of minor skirmishes that had culminated in one big explosion. Tom had been sullen and laconic—not saying much to her or anyone else at their table, even when prompted. He'd kept drinking, even though he was sup-posed to be the one driving them home that night, and when April had suggested that he stop—or at least slow down—Tom had snapped at her. They'd argued with each other right there at the table, while their friends grew increasingly uncomfortable. Tom had insisted that he knew his limits, and said that April should quit trying to be his mother.

She'd eventually managed to get him to quiet down, and had then tried to cheer him up, but none of her efforts worked. He hadn't wanted to dance, not even when the DJ began playing classic rock instead of hip hop. She'd usually been able to count on him to at least shuffle along to AC-DC, Jackyl, or Kix, but not this time. Flirting with him produced no response, either. He'd also made clear his annoyance with some of her friends, especially Tammy, repeatedly throughout the night.

That had led to a discussion on the drive home—a drive which had been harrowing to begin with given Tom's level of inebriation. She'd told him she was upset about his behavior that evening, and about his apparent dislike for Tammy. She was April's best friend, after all, and was supposed to be April's Maid of Honor should they ever get married. Then April brought up her dissatisfaction and insecurities about their prolonged engagement. It had been a little over four years since Tom had popped the question, yet they were still no closer to setting a date. Tom had responded that he was having second thoughts, which then led to crying and shouting. April wasn't sure, but she thought she might have slapped him at some point during that altercation, as well.

The argument ultimately culminated in Tom pulling over on Route 441, halfway between Columbia and Marietta near Chickies Rock County Park, and telling her to get the fuck out of the car. April had, thinking she was calling his bluff. She'd been certain that he'd renege—that he'd apologize and break down and communicate what was really going on with him, and then they'd go home and hold each other and make love. These hopes faded as she watched his taillights rise up over the hill and disappear into the darkness.

April sat down on the guard rail along the side of the road and waited.

Tom didn't come back.

Hurt gave way to anger. She was too mad to cry or pout. She decided to call a friend, but then realized that her cell phone was in her purse—which was behind the passenger seat in Tom's car. Cursing, she stood up and nearly toppled over the guardrail as her head spun. Teetering, she sat back down with a sigh.

"Jesus, I'm fucked up."

She'd wondered what time it was. Last call had been at one o'clock and they'd left the Burning Bridge shortly after that. There was no other traffic on the road. She'd heard a few cars and trucks in the distance, rumbling across the Route 30 bridge that spanned the Susquehanna River, but none of them came her way. Route 441 wasn't nearly as busy as Route 30 was this time of night. Hidden somewhere in the trees above, a dove called out to her, questioning. She'd shouted at it to shut up.

April didn't know how long she'd stayed there, swaying

drunkenly back and forth and alternating between bouts of cursing, crying, and shouting for Tom. At one point, she thought she heard a helicopter, but there was nothing overhead. A few minutes later, she thought she heard people hollering somewhere in the forest, but that sound faded, too. Then, the silence was filled once more with the sounds of nocturnal insects.

Eventually, she'd heard the sound of an engine. Then headlights appeared at the bottom of the hill. She stood up, intent on flagging the vehicle down, but then decided better of it. What if the driver were a serial killer or something? Part of her had known this was unreasonable, but tequila and distress overrode her logic. After all, it wasn't like serial killers were unheard of in Central Pennsylvania. There was that guy from Hanover back in the early Nineties who'd killed all those children in his home and burned their remains in a barrel in his backyard. And of course, everyone knew about the Exit—a notorious killer who'd slain many along Interstate 83 in both Pennsylvania and Maryland before apparently moving on to other highways.

The car was almost upon her when April jumped over the guardrail and stumbled into the woods. Hiding in the tree line, she'd watched it go past, until its taillights vanished just as Tom's had done.

For a brief second, she heard an electronic squawk from somewhere in the woods, as if someone had keyed a radio or walkie-talkie. This was followed by a dim metallic clang, and a feint, unintelligible voice. She couldn't tell if the person was shouting or screaming. When the noises weren't repeated, she decided that she must have either imagined them, or they'd come from farther away, perhaps Columbia or Marietta. Sound traveled strangely at night, especially in these hills.

Then, April promptly forgot all about the strange noises and threw up.

When she was finished vomiting, April felt even worse. Deciding that she was too drunk to even attempt walking home, she'd opted instead to sleep in the woods near Chickies Rock. There were well-marked hiking trails in the forest, and she'd figured if she stuck close to those, she'd be okay. It had been years since she'd actually visited the four hundred and twenty-two acre park, but she remembered there was a gazebo located somewhere within, overlooking the Susquehanna River. With luck, maybe she could find that. She was grateful that it was early-September, and the weather was still relatively nice. Her situation would have been much more perilous had she been stuck out here during the winter months.

She'd tried to think if there was anything else she knew about the location. Its most popular feature was the eponymous rock—a massive outcropping of quartzite that towered over a hundred feet above the Susquehanna River. People standing atop it could see the shore of York County, parts of the little town of Marietta, and the rolling farmlands of northwestern Lancaster County. If she remembered correctly, there were a few playgrounds and some historical markers referring to events that had taken place there during the Civil War.

She'd resolved to hunt for the gazebo and spend the night there. Even if she couldn't sleep, she reasoned, at the very least she could rest until dawn, and then walk back to Columbia and call for help. But fatigue, depression, and alcohol had soon weakened her resolve, and rather than venturing through the dark woods alone, April had decided to stay close to Route 441. She found an area not far from the road that was flat and relatively soft, and nestled up with her back against a tree trunk. She'd tried to ignore the insects crawling around—and sometimes on—her, and tried as well to ignore the sounds of the forest.

Until those sounds had gone quiet.

That had been her first indication that something was wrong, and thinking about it now, she should have run then. She should have hightailed it back to the road as soon as the animals and birds and insects had stopped their chatter. But she hadn't. And instead...

Instead that *thing* had found her.

April heard the creature before she saw it. Twigs and branches snapped under its feet, and it made a strange grunting, snuffling sound, as if it was sniffing the air. She'd seen a shadow, moving between the trees, and assumed it was a bear. She'd watched, helpless, as the form moved toward her. She'd been paralyzed with fear, unable to do anything but whimper softly. In the back of her mind, she'd recalled something her father and brothers (avid hunters all three of them) had once said—if you were approached by a bear in the woods, the best thing to do was to play dead.

But then the thing had stepped into the clearing, walking upright on two legs, and April saw that it wasn't a bear at all. The creature stood about five feet tall and was covered in thick, curly, brown hair. It stank, emitting a musky, sour odor that had filled the clearing. It had a small head with a sloped brow, but a large mouth and a bizarre, oversized jaw that seemed to jut from its face. Despite its short stature, the thing's chest and arms were muscled and broad. Its long fingers and broad feet were tipped with curved, black, mud-caked talons.

April opened her mouth to scream, and the beast had held out one hand, silencing her. Then it grunted and hooted softly, as if trying to speak. When April tried to scurry away, crawling backward on her hands like a crab, it hissed, baring yellowish-white teeth. They'd reminded her of a cross between those of a human and a gorilla.

The thing moved quickly, crossing the distance between them in two quick strides. Before she could escape, it had grasped her feet with both hands. Its nails raked her flesh, digging through her socks and shoes. Grinning, the creature raised its muzzle and sniffed the air. It had tried speaking to her again, but April responded with a shriek. She'd lashed out, kicking with all her might. When the monster loosed its grip, she jumped to her feet. Her victory had been short lived, however, as it dropped her to the ground again with a backhanded swipe across her face. The blow had stunned her, and her vision had momentarily clouded with tears of pain. Then it had fallen on her, shredding and tearing her clothes, and grunting with evident excitement.

April screamed again when she saw the erection between the beast's legs. The swollen member had jutted into the air like a baton, and two tangerine-sized testicles swayed beneath it. She'd aimed her next kick right for them, and when she connected, it was the creature's turn to scream. It toppled backward and the breath rushed from its lungs. April had grimaced at the stench. The monster writhed on the ground, curled into a ball. Then she was on her feet and running.

Which was how she'd ended up here.

But she still didn't know where *here* was.

And that urge to pee had not subsided. Neither had her urge to scream.

She felt around on the ground, searching for something she could use as a weapon. Her fingers closed around a fallen tree branch that was thick enough to use as a club, but the wood was rotten and damp, and fell apart as soon as she picked it up. She continued searching and spotted something glinting at her feet. It appeared to be small and metallic. In her hurry to hide, she must have kicked leaves over the object. She brushed them away and discovered that the item wasn't metallic, but plastic—a laminated security badge of some kind. She squinted, trying to read it in the moonlight filtering through the treetops. The left side of the card had a photo of a man. The right side had what she presumed was his name, Rajic Singh. Below that was a bar code, a series of numbers, and the ubiquitous logo of the Globe Corporation. The ID card was in good shape. April wondered how it had gotten out here, in the woods, and where its owner was. Maybe he was camping or hiking nearby. Maybe he'd heard her screams and was coming to help.

And maybe as soon as he did, the beast would lunge out from behind a tree and rip him to shreds.

Maybe the monster already had.

She stuck the identification card in her back pocket, and tried once more to think. The woods were still quiet. If the beast was nearby, it was staying hidden. Shuddering, April debated whether to stay where she was, or make a break for it. While she was still trying to decide, she heard a rumbling sound in the distance—a tractor-trailer, the driver downshifting as the big truck trundled up the hill on Route 441. That meant that the road had to be nearby!

Abandoning caution, April sprang to her feet and rushed toward the sound. Her chest felt tight and her breathing was ragged. Her face had swollen from the monster's blow, and she was beginning to feel the pain from all the cuts and scratches she'd incurred while trying to escape. Her blood had grown sticky, and there were bits of leaves and bark and dirt in her wounds. She heard the truck's gears grind, but it seemed to be behind her now. She spun around, disoriented.

"Wait," she shouted. "Help me!"

April was immediately dismayed by her stupidity. Yes, she was drunk, and yes, she had shouted out of desperation and despair, but it had been an appalling act of bad judgment.

Her need to pee was insistent now, causing her sides to ache and throb. She stifled a moan.

A branch snapped to her right, followed by another. April turned her head in that direction. Two small maple saplings bent aside as her pursuer pushed his way through them. Spotting her, the creature raised his head to the night sky and roared.

"No," April moaned. "Leave me alone, goddamn it!"

Shrieking, April turned and fled again, all-too-aware that she was now running away from where she guessed the road was. She didn't care. All that mattered was getting away from her attacker. She cried aloud with joy as the terrain changed beneath her feet. Rather than running through the detritus of the forest floor, she now found herself on one of the park's many hiking trails. Her progress immediately grew easier now that she wasn't ducking branches and shrugging off vines and tripping over roots and stones.

Clouds passed over the moon, and the woods grew dark, but April barely noticed. The only thing she was aware of was the angry, determined sound of pursuit behind her. She stuck to the trail, and thought she might actually be managing to outdistance the creature. She vaulted over an obstacle in the dark. She wasn't sure what it was. A fallen tree or a railing or maybe a fence, perhaps. She stumbled on the other side, but then regained her balance. As she started running again, she risked a glance over her shoulder.

Then the ground disappeared from beneath her feet, and April fell, too startled to even scream.

The moon came out from behind the clouds again, but April was gone.

TWO

Levi Stoltzfus sat at the writing desk in his study, which was a room located in the center of his small, one-story house. A lone lamp with a single, naked bulb provided the only illumination, barely beating back the shadows. The room's four walls had built-in bookshelves that spanned from floor to ceiling. They overflowed with old, unabridged occult and esoteric books—the *Book of Soyga*, the collected works of John Dee, Guido von List's *Das Geheimnis der Runen*, the original, unabridged version of Frazer's *The Golden Bough,* Francis Barrett's *The Magus*, the *Cipher Manuscripts* (including the Johannes Trithemius cipher), Johann Scheible's *Das Kloster*, Cyril Scott's *The Initiate*, Parkes' *Fourth Book of Agrippa*, all of Aleister Crowley's occult work, and many more. Normally, Levi enjoyed spending time in the room, leisurely perusing the books (or more recently, through his eBook reader), but tonight, he barely noticed them.

Levi's brow furrowed in deep concentration as he pored over a stack of papers that had been photocopied from the archives of the Historical Society of Schuylkill County. He was reading the account of a man named Heim, who had served with Captain Morgan at Fort Lebanon and had apparently used powwow magic to defend against the native Indians of the time. That wasn't the part that kept Levi reading, even as his eyes grew itchy and tired, and fatigue set in for the night. He knew all about powwow magic, being a practitioner of it himself. It wasn't even Heim that interested

Levi. He had known of the man before now. Levi's father and grandfather had recounted Heim's exploits to him when he was younger—before Levi's excommunication from their Amish community. All of this was old news, as far as Levi was concerned.

What he was really looking for was any account of Heim doing battle locally with a demon from the Judeo-Christian pantheon—a particular demon named Abalam, one of the many such creatures that made up the host collectively referred to as Legion, and a servant of the arch-demon Paimon.

A month ago, Levi had been called upon to assist a nearby local police department with a multiple murder investigation that had involved a distinctly paranormal bent. It had started with a possessed tree—one inhabited by Abalam. Levi had attempted an exorcism of the tree, but when his efforts proved fruitless, and Abalam refused to leave, Levi had been forced to quite literally make a deal with a devil. He called upon Abalam's master, the great Paimon, and asked a boon. In exchange for Abalam being sent back to Hell and bothering the people of Earth no more, Levi was indebted to Paimon. The arch-demon could call upon Levi's services.

"It would have to be at a time of my choosing," Paimon had said. *"You shall not know the hour, nor the task, until it is at hand."*

Out of options, Levi had reluctantly agreed to the arch-demon's terms. And now, a month later, he was troubled. His distress did not stem only from the fact that he was now essentially on call for one of the most powerful beings in Hell. What troubled him more than this was the fact that he'd been put in such a situation in the first place. His exorcism—something which should have been almost routine to a magus with Levi's capabilities—had utterly failed. For the first time in his life, for the first time since he had been called to this form of servitude, it had felt to Levi that God had deserted him. When he had called upon the power of the Holy Spirit, there had been no response. But why?

Both Abalam and Paimon had taunted Levi with a riddle before their departure. They had told him that Heaven was in disarray. Paimon had taunted Levi with a rumor that the Holy Trinity had been torn asunder, and that the walls of the Labyrinth—a mystical dimension that tied reality itself together—were growing thin and collapsing. The demon had warned Levi that the end of times were almost at hand.

Levi had pondered all of this in the weeks since then, wondering what it meant for him, and more importantly, for the world. He'd reached out to others in his network, a wide and varied array of occultists, scholars, clergy, and freelancers like himself, all serving or knowledgeable in a multitude of religions, deities, demons, and magical theories and practices. Their differences in beliefs didn't matter. They all answered to a higher purpose. Rabbis, Satanists, bishops, death cults, Baptists, shamans, pujaris, mediums, Thelemites, fellow powwow practitioners, faith-healers, parapsychologists, demonologists, and even a madman who claimed to have lived for a time among a prehistoric aquatic race of intelligent reptilian beings known as the Dark Ones—Levi had communicated with them all, and what he'd learned only increased his dismay.

Something was wrong. Everyone agreed on that. They also concurred a general feeling that something was coming. But the identity of that something was where they differed. Some thought it was an event. Some theories involved a global apocalypse triggered by a natural disaster such as an asteroid strike or pole shift. Others thought the apocalypse would be anything but natural, and spoke to more supernatural ends of the Earth via the emergence of Leviathan or the Siqqusim or some other other-worldly entity or race. A few thought the end might simply be a transformation or a trigger that would elevate humanity. These individuals proposed it might involve the return of various religious figures and the fulfillment of prophesies involving everyone from Jesus to Quetzalcoatl to Romulus to Bodhidharma, which would in turn lead to everything from the Rapture to the Yawm al-Qiyāmah. But these positive thinkers, as Levi had begun to refer to them, were in the distinct minority. Most of his peers, while disagreeing on the exact nature of the threat, felt assured that something bad was coming.

Unfortunately, Levi was no closer to figuring out what that something was, and this only served to strengthen his unease. That was why he'd turned to the past, rather than divining the present, hoping that if he discovered how Abalam and Paimon had been defeated in the past, it might give him leverage over the arch-demon, and thus, Levi might be able to force Paimon to reveal to him what was really going on. So far, however, his research had been to no avail. He already knew that Abalam had ended up in the tree after a 1909 exorcism by a powwow practitioner known as Rehmeyer. He had hoped he might find an earlier account of Abalam, or one of the other members of the Legion, menacing the region. But there was none.

Frustrated, Levi closed his eyes and pinched the bridge of his nose. He sighed, wondering what to do next. His thoughts then wandered to the pain in his lower back. Levi would turn thirty-six later this year, but recently, he'd felt much older. He seemed to ache more, and he was slower to wake in the morning and grew tired more quickly at night. Perhaps it was just his lifestyle catching up with him. In the seventeen years since he'd been excommunicated by his church and ostracized by his community and family, he'd seen a lot—traveling the world, and serving where needed. Sometimes, the price of that servitude was high, but so far he'd born it well. It helped that he always had this house to return to, an operational center that was as much a part of him as anything else. In many ways, the home was where his heart truly lay, and he always found it a comfort when, returning from some far off location, he saw it waiting for him. He supposed that he should really get around to buying the property outright, rather than renting. But these days, even the house seemed unsettling, almost as if it, too, felt that there was something amiss.

He opened his eyes and let his gaze wander around the room, settling on a framed photograph which sat nestled on one of the many bookshelves throughout the house. The picture frame was wedged between several hardcover occult texts and a small, gilded silver pillbox. The box contained the fangs of a vampire that had haunted the sewers and maintenance tunnels beneath Pittsburgh. The photograph was of Levi and two men who had helped him dispatch the vampire. The first was Taggert—an accomplished painter and a powerful Hemomancer. Taggert had lost his life in the final battle with the vampire, although Levi still heard from him occasionally. The second man in the picture was a chaos magician named Dez. Levi and Dez had been close once—as close as those in their particular profession could be. Unlike Taggert, Dez was still alive, but it had been a long time since Levi had seen his friend. Indeed, he heard from Taggert more often.

He'd reached out to Dez just a week ago, making the same inquiries he'd made of others in their occult circles, but so far, Dez hadn't responded. Levi supposed he could be too busy to check his email. Dez had always been eccentric, and there had been times in the past when he'd dropped out of contact for months at a time. Also, Dez had recently moved to Columbus, Ohio. Levi supposed that Dez could be preoccupied with unpacking and adjusting to his new home, but his gut told him that wasn't the case—and Levi's gut instincts were rarely wrong.

"Your will be done, Lord," he prayed aloud. "But it would be a lot easier if I knew just what that will of Yours entailed. You sent Moses a burning bush. Is it too much for me to ask for a text message on occasion?"

As usual, there was no response.

Levi shrugged. "Sorry, Lord. If I'm meant to unravel Paimon's riddle and free myself from this debt, then that's what will happen. And if not, then it probably won't matter anyway."

His words seemed to hang there in the silence. Levi pushed his chair back and stood up from the desk. His prayers and thoughts of Dez were momentarily pushed aside by a memory—an image of a girl running through a cornfield and laughing, urging a much younger version of himself to give chase. She promised that if he caught her, he could have her, and he meant to do both. The girl's name was Rebecca. She'd been his first—and only—love.

"Why now?" Levi ground his teeth. "Why show me this now, Lord?"

Then, as it always did, the memory flashed forward, and Rebecca was no longer running or laughing. Instead, she was laying on the ground between the rows, split open from crotch to sternum. Her knit bonnet had been knocked from her head, and there was corn silk, twigs, and dirt in her long blonde hair. And also blood.

Lots of blood.

The cornstalks rustled, but there was no wind. Laughter

erupted, seeming to come from the air, the ground, nowhere and everywhere. It was a demon's laugh, but Levi barely noticed it. He was still staring at the blood. It covered the ground around Rebecca, seeping into the cracks in the dry earth. Blood coated her shredded dress—and her equally mangled skin. And her...

"Stop it!" Rocking back and forth on his feet as if slapped, Levi balled his fists and rubbed his eyes. When he opened them again, the vision was gone.

"Is that it? Was I damned back then, Lord? Is this just payback now? Has my penance finally come due?"

Again, if the Lord answered, Levi didn't hear the reply.

He stood there for a moment, fighting the urge to sob. The memories of that fateful summer when everything had changed and he'd learned just what high a price magic had, threatened to overwhelm him again. He willed them away, trying not to think about what he'd lost—the only girl he'd ever loved, his family, his community.

His soul?

"No," he whispered. "At least, not yet."

Eventually, the moment passed. The grief and self-pity receded back under the surface of his psyche again. Levi took another deep breath and tried to steel himself.

"Right," he said. "I've been looking to the past all evening. It's no wonder I am remembering the past, as well. I should break from this for a while. Perhaps do some woodworking."

Most of Levi's neighbors in the small town of Marietta thought that he was simply a woodworker. Half of the two-car garage at the rear of his property had been converted into a wood shop. The other half of the garage was used as a stable for his horse, Dee—named after the infamous John Dee, one of the greatest magical practitioners who had ever lived, and an associate of Levi's ancestors. During the week, when he wasn't otherwise engaged, Levi spent a few hours each day out in the wood shop, crafting various goods—coat and spoon racks, chairs, tables, dressers, and other things out of wood. Then, on Saturdays, he hauled them in his buggy to the local flea market. The money he earned from this paid for his rent, groceries, and utilities.

A few of Levi's neighbors knew about his other, more secret vocation. He worked a type of magic and faith healing called powwow, as had his father and grandfather before him. Often, locals sought him out for medical treatments and alternative medicine. His patients were usually the elderly (who still remembered the old ways), the poor (who didn't have health insurance or who couldn't afford to see a doctor), and people who preferred a more holistic approach to their health. Patients came to Levi seeking treatments for everything from the flu to arthritis. Occasionally, he was called upon for more serious matters such as stopping bleeding or mending a broken bone.

But powwow went beyond medicine. It was a magical discipline just like any other, and quite often, Levi was charged with facing threats that were supernatural, rather than biological, in origin. Exorcisms, telepathy, lycanthropy, dimensional portals, hauntings, even necromancy—Levi had been called upon to deal with some strange things in his career. He'd been called many things. Magus. Occult detective. Paranormal investigator. Ghost hunter. Supernatural historian. Exorcist. Witch and warlock.

But for right now, he didn't want to be that person. He thought that instead, he'd prefer to leave the occult behind for an evening and just work in the solace of his wood shop. It was an activity that never failed to bring him comfort and peace, and he was in desperate need of both tonight.

As Levi left his study and walked down the hall, his cell phone rang. Like his buggy, style of dress, and other factors in his life, the cell phone often confused those who mistakenly assumed that Levi was still Amish. He sometimes asked them what they expected him to use instead, to stay in touch with people. Carrier pigeons and ham radios didn't seem very practical, and divination and necromancy weren't his preferred method of speaking to a utility company's customer service representative or a dear friend just calling to say hello. The same went for telepathy, which always gave him nosebleeds.

Levi pulled the cell phone from his pocket and saw that Sterling Myers, his next door neighbor, was calling. Sterling was a good man. He was a decade older than Levi, married and still in love with his wife (if somewhat begrudgingly), and had two kids (one in college and the other a senior in high school). Sterling was gregarious by nature, and always willing to carry on a conversation. Indeed, Sterling could talk all night, if given the opportunity, which sometimes proved an annoyance. But Levi was grateful for the older man. Sterling could always be counted on to feed and care for Levi's dog, Crowley (named after Aleister Crowley, another associate of Levi's ancestors). When necessity dictated that Levi travel by automobile, plane, or train, Sterling also looked after Dee. He was one of a dozen people whom Levi implicitly trusted, and one of the few friends Levi had outside of occult social circles.

Levi answered the phone. "Hello, Sterling."

"Heya, Levi. Didn't wake you, did I?"

"No, not at all. I could use a break, actually. I was just heading outside to do some woodwork."

"Well…" Sterling stalled, clearing his throat. "I hate to interrupt."

"It's fine, Sterling. Please. How may I assist you?"

"It's just that… I've got a buddy of mine here. He really needs to talk to you. You know what I mean?"

"Of course. I'll be happy to help, if I can. What ails him?"

"Oh, he's not sick, Levi. Well, I mean, other than the fact that he's a Ravens fan. But hell, anybody that would root for Baltimore has to be a little sick in the head, you know? I mean, I love the Orioles, but those Ravens are nothing but thugs."

Levi smiled, but said nothing. Normally, he grew impatient when Sterling began to ramble, but tonight, he was enjoying the digression. It felt normal. And he desperately needed a sense of normalcy.

"Anyway," Sterling continued, "he doesn't need a powwow doctor. That's not why I'm calling. He needs… well, you do other stuff. That paranormal shit. He needs to talk to somebody who knows about those things."

"I see."

Levi's pulse quickened. The last time Sterling had called him under similar circumstances, it had involved a York County plainclothes detective, which had ultimately led to Levi's confrontation with Abalam and Paimon. Levi was adept in many different—and at times conflicting—schools of magic, including the often misunderstood art of synchronicity magic. He recognized synchronicity when it happened. It was happening now. Things were aligning. A path had been set before him, and though he didn't know where it would lead, he had no choice but to follow.

"I'll be over shortly," he said. "I just need to take care of a few things first."

Before leaving the house, Levi washed up and got dressed. He was dismayed to notice a white strand of hair in his long, well-kept beard. This wasn't the first such hair he'd found over the last few months, but it was the most prominent—the others having been hidden amongst the thatch on his chest and arms. After scrubbing his face and toweling off, he put on black pants and shoes, a white button-down shirt, and suspenders. He paused for a moment in front of the bedroom closet, trying to decide between a black dress coat or a black vest with many pockets. He opted for the latter, reasoning that it was warm outside, and—depending on what the encounter with Sterling's friend led to—he might need the vest's pockets to carry various items. Levi noticed that the vest, which had been snug around his waist just a month before, now hung loose. He reminded himself to start eating more. Then he wondered if it would really matter if he did. Unless he soon dealt with Paimon's riddle, weight loss would be the least of his worries.

On his way out, Levi stopped in the foyer and collected a small, battered volume from the table. The dog-eared book was his copy of *The Long Lost Friend*—a family heirloom, and the primary tool of someone in his line of work. The book had once belonged to Levi's father, Amos, and his grandfather before him. It was small enough to slip into one of his vest pockets, which he did, sliding it over his heart. Levi never left home without the book. It was his most important possession—the first thing he'd grab if there were ever a fire. Unlike the public domain versions of the book sold online and in New Age bookstores, Levi's edition of *The Long Lost Friend* was unabridged, and contained many long-unpublished spells. It provided valuable protection against certain enemies and dangers. The front page had the following inscription: *Whoever carries this book with him is safe from all his enemies, visible or invisible; and whoever has this book with him cannot die without the holy corpse of Jesus Christ, nor be drowned in any water, nor burn up in*

any fire, nor can any unjust sentence be passed upon him.
The book had saved Levi from harm countless times, but he
hoped that he wouldn't need it tonight.

Almost as an afterthought, he grabbed his favorite wide-
brimmed straw hat from a hook on the wall and perched it
atop his head, poking a few stray curls of hair beneath the
brim with his finger.

"I'm going out," he told the silent, invisible guardian who
watched over his home. "Behave yourself until I return."

The air shifted around him, indicating the guardian's
presence. After sensing that it understood, Levi opened the
door and stepped outside. He crossed the yard, and—after
looking both ways—the street. Seeing his master leaving,
Crowley whined from his pen, looking after him with
mournful eyes.

"I'll be right back," Levi called, deciding he'd take the
dog for a walk later. They could both use it, he thought.
It had been weeks since he'd spent any quality time with
Crowley or Dee, absorbed in his research as he'd been, and
Levi resolved to do better.

He was still thinking about it, and feeling guilty, as he
strode up Sterling's sidewalk. Before he could reach the
porch, the front door opened and Sterling stepped outside,
followed by a man Levi didn't recognize. He was about
the same age as Levi, sported a thick, unruly shock of red
hair, spectacularly freckled, and in good physical shape. His
troubled eyes were dark brown, and his stature indicated that
of a man with the weight of the world on his shoulders. Even
his aura projected it. This was a man who was troubled by
something.

"Heya, Levi." Sterling let the screen door slam shut
behind them. "Thanks for coming over. This is my friend,
John. He's a volunteer with the fire company."

Sterling leaned against the porch rail and lit a cigarette. John took two tentative steps down the stairs. Levi crossed the distance between them and stuck out his hand. John shook it. Levi noticed the man's palm was damp.

"Nice to meet you, Mr. Stoltzfus," John said.

"You may call me Levi, if you like." He smiled reassuringly and then dropped John's hand. "Sterling said you had a problem I might be able to help with?"

John sighed. He glanced at Sterling and then back to Levi. Shuffling from one foot to the other, he then put his hands in his pockets and stared at the ground.

"I do," he muttered, "but it sounds crazy."

"I deal with crazy all the time," Levi said. "Try me."

Slowly, John glanced upward and met his gaze. Levi did his best to project calm. It was an easy task—the simplest of all magic. And what was magic, really, if not simply projecting ones will upon others? His efforts were rewarded a moment later as John visibly relaxed.

"Well," John began, "I'm a volunteer for the fire company. I'm sure you heard about the girl's body that was found this morning over by Chickies Rock?"

Levi shook his head. "I'm afraid that I haven't. I've been working all day and into this evening. I haven't had the news or radio on, and I wasn't on any of the news sites online."

John frowned. "I thought Amish people couldn't own televisions and computers?"

"I told you." Sterling exhaled smoke and coughed. "Levi ain't Amish no more."

"Sterling is correct," Levi said. "I was Amish, but it has been quite some time since I left that community. But please, continue. I take it your problem has something to do with this body you mentioned?"

"Yeah," John replied. "That's where it starts, at least.

101

Early this morning, some fishermen found a girl's body below Chickies Rock, right between the railroad tracks and the river. They called 911, and I was on duty so we headed over. Got there before the police or the EMTs. Wasn't much anybody could have done for her. She was…I've never seen anything like that before. I mean, I've seen some bad shit. Terrible shit. There was a house fire two years ago, and a little kid got burned real bad. That was terrible. But this girl…her body. It was pretty obvious she'd fallen from the top. I imagine you've been to Chickies Rock before? If so, you know how far of a drop that is."

Levi did indeed. Given that the park was only a mile and a half south of town, he'd gone hiking there many times, admiring the extensive view the cliff face offered on clear days.

"About a hundred feet, if I recall correctly. But aren't there hand rails to keep visitors back from the edge of the cliff?"

John shrugged. "Yeah, there are. But some of them aren't in great shape, and there's one spot—a corner ledge—that doesn't have any railings at all."

"So this young woman somehow made it past those fell a hundred feet."

John nodded. "And not into the river, either. It's hard to see from the top, unless you're clinging to the cliff itself, but the drop leads down to the railroad tracks. You'd have to jump out from the cliff a good thirty feet or so before you'd hit the water."

"And I take it this young lady landed on the railroad tracks?"

"Yeah," John said. "Well, at first she did. They think she must have…bounced. Her body just sort of came apart on impact. And then parts of her landed elsewhere. Animals had been at her, too."

The volunteer fireman paused, clearly struggling with his emotions. Levi waited, allowing the man to regain his composure. Coughing again, Sterling snuffed out his cigarette and shifted from foot to foot. When John continued with his story, his voice was quieter, almost a monotone.

"We…we were among the first to arrive. Wasn't too hard to find her. We could smell her before we came on the site. And we had to chase off a few turkey buzzards that were… well, you know."

Levi nodded encouragement.

"Anyway, we secured the scene until the cops showed up. Then they took over and kept everyone back until the homicide detectives arrived. The site was closed down most of the day. They only carted her off a few hours ago."

"Was it a suicide?"

"That's what we heard the coroner and the detectives are going to rule it as. And that's why Sterling said I should talk to you."

"You don't think it was suicide or an accidental fall?"

"I don't know," John admitted. "But what I do know is that there's something weird going on."

"How so?"

"Well, three things. First of all, a buddy of mine from the fire-house says they found a footprint at the top of the cliff. And it wasn't human. I know it sounds like bullshit, but this guy has no reason to lie. He said it was like Bigfoot."

Levi frowned. "An Albatwitch, perhaps?"

"I don't know what that is," John said.

"I do!" Sterling sounded excited for the opportunity to contribute to the conversation. "It's a Pennsylvania Dutch name. Means 'apple thief' or something. Supposed to be a Bigfoot. Right, Levi?"

"Apple snitch, actually," Levi corrected him. "And although they weren't Sasquatch—at least, not like the popular description of Sasquatch—they may very well have been a cousin. Albatwitches were much shorter. Usually around four feet tall, although there were a few reports of them reaching as high as five feet in stature."

"I never heard of them," John said.

"I'm surprised," Levi replied. "They are a big part of local folklore. But, I guess like so many other things today, the old ways and tales are no longer taught."

"My kids don't know what a cassette tape is," Sterling said, "let alone a record album. They thought it was just a big CD."

Levi focused on John. "It is said they've always been here, living in the woods along the shore in Columbia and Marietta, as well as on the York County side of the river. The main tribe of creatures were centered in and around Chickies Rock. They stayed up in the trees, mostly, descending only to forage for food. As you might guess from their name, they had a particular fondness for apples. They used to steal them from farms, and there are even some accounts of them sneaking apples from picnickers and tossing the cores back down from the treetops. So you can understand why the Dutch settlers called them Albatwitches."

"Not many apple trees around here," John said. "Especially not around Chickies Rock."

"No," Levi agreed. "There aren't. At least, not these days. But when this area was first settled, there were apple trees on every farm. They were a staple of the pioneers. Hardy, easy to grow, and adaptable. You could make everything from jam to pies to moonshine out of them. They canned well enough to store for winter. And the woods were full of wild apples, back then, as well."

"Did they ever attack anybody?" John asked.

Sterling frowned. "The apples?"

"No, you idiot." John sighed. "I mean the Albatwitches."

Levi shook his head. "I have never read of them doing so, and believe me, I've studied them at length. They were scary to look at, I'm sure. The Susquehannock tribes reportedly adorned their shields with carven images of an Albatwitch, to create fear in their enemies. But the creatures themselves were not fierce in nature. I imagine their diet was mostly apples and other fruits. They never harmed anyone, judging by the available accounts. Their primary defense seems to have been a sound they made with their tails—a noise like a whip cracking."

Sterling lit another cigarette. "Appletarian or not, I still wouldn't want to come across one in the dark."

Levi shrugged. "I've encountered worse."

"I'll bet you have," Sterling agreed, "and I don't want to know."

Seconds after he said it, Levi was puzzled by his own admission. He was not in the habit of sharing details of his work with anyone, especially those he considered 'civilians'. Names and information were power, and although he trusted Sterling more than most, Levi knew all-too-well what could happen if information, no matter how seemingly vague or trivial, ended up in the wrong hands. He wondered what had possessed him to admit such a thing to Sterling, especially in the presence of someone like John. Fear of the future? His weariness of going through life alone? Other as yet unseen or unknown forces? Or was he simply exhausted from his studies, and had accidentally let something slip?

"You're right, Sterling," Levi murmured. "You don't want to know."

Sterling's tone was sympathetic. "But I don't guess

you'll run into an Albatwitch. They were supposed to have gone extinct in the early 1900s."

"That is what the legends say," Levi agreed, "but there have been sightings since then. There were several in the 1950s and 1970s, and two more in 2005 and 2008."

"At Chickies Rock?" Sterling asked.

"A few. The more recent ones were across the river, in York County. One in the town of Red Lion and another in Wrightsville."

"Out near LeHorn's Hollow," John said. "Where they have that Goat-Man legend? Same thing?"

For a brief moment, Levi's visage darkened. "No. The Goat-Man is something very different. And that particular bit of folklore is most certainly extinct."

"How do you know? Is that part of…what you do? Your job?"

"It is. But you said there were three things that concerned you, John. You mentioned the footprint. What else has occurred?"

"Well, the cops are hushing up the footprint. They told us they didn't want a bunch of whackos showing up and tramping around the site. But not even a half hour after they said this, that documentary crew from Cryptid Hunter showed up at the park. Had their cameras and everything. The cops didn't let them anywhere near where the girl had fallen, but still, it was weird that they got there so quick. Kind of like they'd been closer than we knew. They looked really nervous, too."

"I'm afraid that I am not familiar with Cryptid Hunter," Levi said. "I assume it's a television show?"

"Yeah," Sterling said. "They run around every week looking for monsters. Never find anything, though. Hell, Levi, you need to pay more attention to the local news.

They've been over the river in York County all week, filming a special on Scratch."

"I hadn't heard," Levi admitted. "But I know of Scratch, of course. The legendary giant water snake. My father used to tease us with tales of him when we were young."

John sighed. "Scratch, the Goat-Man, and now this Albatwitch thing. If I hadn't seen what I saw today, I wouldn't believe any of it."

"Did you see the footprint for yourself?" Levi asked.

"No. None of us on the ground did. And I doubt anyone will now."

"Why is that?"

"That's the third thing I wanted to tell you. The part that really freaked me out. Just before they removed the girl's body, these security goons showed up."

Levi frowned. "The State Police?"

"No," John said. "A bunch of fucking mercenaries from Globe Security."

"Globe?" Levi's frown increased. "They're a private security contractor. I thought they only hired out for places like Afghanistan and Iraq. This is a local law enforcement matter. What are they doing at Chickies Rock?"

"Your guess is as good as mine," John said. "But they've set up a perimeter, and they're not letting anybody into the park. Even the cops seemed kind of surprised that they were there. I asked my Chief, and he says the order came from higher up, and I should stop asking questions. And that's bullshit. It's bad enough they hushed up that footprint, but now this? There's something weird going on."

"And I told him you're good with weird," Sterling said. "So, what do you think, Levi? Is it worth checking out?"

Levi smiled, trying to hide his concern, and then shrugged.

"I suppose I could look into it."

THREE

In the hour between dusk and dark, Levi made preparations. He began by placing a call to his friend Maria, a reporter for one of York County's two newspapers. She made some calls to a colleague who wrote for the Lancaster newspaper, and confirmed for Levi that something had indeed been found atop Chickies Rock, overlooking where the girl had fallen. But while John had seemed to think there was only one footprint, Maria's source told her there had been dozens. Some of them had no doubt belonged to the victim, identified as April Nace. But the other prints were what Levi was most interested in. Maria told him they were shaped like a human's, with five toes, but much larger—at least a foot in length, broad, and apparently tipped with talons or claws of some sort. The newspaper's editor had spiked mention of the footprints, reporting only that the victim had fallen from Chickies Rock, and that authorities were working to determine if it was suicide, accident, or foul play.

Something else Maria told him was a rumor that the detectives had found something in the victim's back pocket—an employee ID card belonging to someone from the Globe Corporation. Unfortunately, she'd been unable to confirm the rumor, and her editor had blocked further attempts to do so, citing orders from the newspaper's publisher.

After hanging up with Maria, Levi was even more puzzled than he'd been when first hearing John recount the details. The presence of Globe personnel was troubling. Their involvement made no sense. But what concerned him more was the footprints found at the top of Chickies Rock. They were far too big to belong to an Albatwitch, which meant something else was on the loose. And he still wasn't convinced that a community of Albatwitches still existed in the area, either. There were reports of a population still living in Nova Scotia, where the Algonquin's called them Megumoowesoos, and he suspected that Florida's infamous Skunk Ape might be a relative, but as far as here at Chickies Rock, he believed them to be extinct.

So what, then, was he dealing with? What could leave a footprint like John and Maria had described, but not be an Albatwitch? There were several possibilities, and none that he relished. A lycanthrope, perhaps, or a demon. Those seemed the most likely suspects. Whatever the nature of the threat, it was a relatively new arrival, as Levi had never sensed its presence during his own sojourns into the county park.

He was then left wondering how best to prepare. He selected a small silver cross with a silver chain, and placed it around his neck, hidden beneath his clothes. He reasoned the silver would prove useful against any were-creature, and the cross itself would be a defense should the threat be a demon of Judeo-Christian origin. He then went to the foyer and chose a walking stick made of ash. The wood itself offered a powerful deterrent against many types of evil, and the staff was solid enough to strike something physically without splintering or snapping. He then filled his vest pockets with various small vials of sage, salt, and other aids. He also kept his copy of *The Long Lost Friend* over his breast—a guaranteed failsafe should other measures fail.

Satisfied with his armament, Levi went out to the garage and hooked Dee to the buggy. The horse neighed and nuzzled him with delight, thrilled with whatever prospect Levi had in store. From his spot in the yard, Crowley leaped and yipped, rattling his chain, begging to come along.

"Don't worry," Levi told the dog, untying him. "I didn't forget about you. A promise is a promise. And besides, I may have need of your tracking skills. We might put that nose of yours to work before the night is through."

Crowley sat next to him on the bench in the buggy, ears up and tongue lolling. Despite his apprehension at the evening's events, Levi couldn't help but grin. The dog's enthusiasm was infectious. He reached over and scratched Crowley's ears. Crowley leaned into the gesture, and his back leg thumped. Still grinning, Levi picked up the reigns and guided Dee out of the garage and onto the road.

He noticed Sterling standing outside on his porch, smoking another cigarette. There was no sign of John. A television flickered behind Sterling's curtains. As Dee clopped past, the neighbor raised his hand and waved.

"Be careful, Levi."

Smiling, Levi returned the gesture. "I always am. The Lord protects those who serve Him."

But as they rounded the corner, and Sterling's house passed from sight, Levi's smile faded.

* * *

Normally, the deserted stretch of Route 441 along which the entrance to the county park was located grew pitch black after dark, illuminated only sporadically by passing headlights or a full moon. But as Dee led them up the hill toward the parking area (with a long line of patient local drivers following behind her, all of whom were accustomed to co-existing in traffic with the slower-moving Amish buggies), Levi noticed a bright glow that bathed the trees in a yellow haze.

Upon cresting the hill, he saw massive floodlights towering over the parking area. Generators hummed, drowning out passing traffic. The lot was full of cars, vans, and trucks, all painted black, and all with the familiar logo of the Globe Corporation emblazoned on their doors. Men and a few women stood beneath the floodlights and between the vehicles. The personnel all wore similarly colored body armor or uniforms, all of which had an identical logo. Levi had seen the body armor on the news—the shields and helmets with dark visors having been a common sight in Iraq, Libya, Afghanistan, Syria, and other places where the mercenaries hired out—but it was unsettling to now see them on display in his small corner of the world. Many of the men were armed with rifles. Several had holstered side-arms, as well. Levi didn't know exactly what types of rifles the security personnel carried. His knowledge of firearms began and ended with the rifles he'd used to hunt small game and deer as a boy—an activity he hadn't engaged in since his banishment from his community. He was fairly certain that whatever their caliber or make, the rifles the Globe Security forces carried weren't optimal for pheasant hunting—unless one intended on turning the pheasant into a fine, red mist.

In addition to the mercenaries, there were three civilians. Judging by the amount of camera equipment they carried, Levi assumed they were part of the Cryptid Hunter television crew that Sterling and John had mentioned. There was a young woman with several visible piercings and tattoos, and a thin young man with glasses and short-cropped hair. Both looked barely out of college. The third man was closer to Levi's age, and was dressed like he was on a safari. The clothing wasn't practical for an early-Autumn stroll through the woods of Central Pennsylvania, but Levi supposed it looked good on television. He noticed that all three seemed frazzled and exhausted. They stood somewhat apart from the Globe team, watching the proceedings, but—curiously—not filming.

He was also struck by the fact that there were no local officials on hand. Surely, for an operation of this magnitude, there should have at least been a few local police cars at the scene, or volunteer fireman directing traffic. Instead, two stern-looking security personnel were performing that duty, grimly waving cars on as passersby slowed down to gawk at the scene.

Levi guided Dee over to the side of the road. Crowley shifted uneasily on the seat beside him. The dog sniffed the air. His ears were flat and his tail stayed firmly between his legs. He sensed something wrong.

Levi sensed it, too.

Traffic continued to creep by. Gravel crunched beneath the buggy's tires. Two guards approached them even before he'd reigned Dee to a complete halt. Neither man carried a rifle, but Levi noticed that they kept their hands near their pistols. As they drew closer, Dee tossed her head and snorted.

"Easy," Levi whispered.

"Sir," one of the guards said, "you need to keep moving. You're blocking traffic."

Levi glanced over his shoulder at the slow-moving line of cars, and then back to the guard. "Traffic seems to be flowing. I can assure you that drivers in this county are quite accustomed to sharing the roads with buggies."

"Be that as it may, sir, your parking along the side here creates a safety hazard for our personnel. I'm asking you to move along."

"Nothing to see here?" Levi grinned.

The guard did not return the gesture. "Exactly."

"I'm sorry," Levi said. "I didn't get your name?"

"And you're not going to, either. I don't answer to you."

"Then who do you answer to? And why the hostility? This is my town. I have a right to know what is occurring in it. Are you with the local police?"

"Clear out, or we'll clear you out, sir. Have a good evening."

The guard turned away from Levi, clearly dismissing him. Levi frowned.

"Excuse me," he called. "I still have a few—"

The man whirled around. His expression was clouded with frustration.

"Sir, I advised you to leave this area. You refused to comply. Now I'm going to tell you one more time. If you still refuse to obey that order, I'll have no choice but to take other measures."

"Oh? Do tell? What might these other measures entail?"

The guard's right hand moved to his weapon. Simultaneously, he raised his left hand to the collar of his shirt. Levi noticed a small, button-sized device clipped to it. The man tilted the device and spoke into it.

"Can I get some back-up over here, please? I've got a gentleman refusing to comply."

He smiled at Levi. It was not a warm, welcoming gesture. Levi thought it looked more like a grimace. Several other uniformed guards began to approach them. The camera crew also seemed to take a sudden interest in what was occurring. Levi felt Crowley tense beside him, his haunches taught and ready.

"Now, sir," the guard said, un-holstering his weapon and eyeing the dog. "I'm going to ask you to step down from your—"

Dee reared back her head and then, with one loud convulsion, sneezed in the guard's face, splattering him with globs of mucous. Sputtering, the guard choked off in mid-sentence and stood there gaping as thick strands of horse snot dripped from his nose and chin. The other approaching guards burst into laughter at their friend's predicament. Stifling a smile, Levi resisted the urge to pat the horse and tell her what a good girl she was.

The other guards were almost upon them now. Crowley growled again. Levi glanced back at traffic, wondering if these men would risk a confrontation in front of so many witnesses. How would it play to the public if a group of private security personnel were seen harassing a seemingly-Amish man? He studied the auras of those approaching, intent on divining their possible demeanor and intentions, but before he could, there was a commotion at the tree line. A forklift trundled out of the woods, shaking and rumbling as its tires dug into the uneven soil. Suspended on the forks was a twisted steel cage. Its frame had buckled and something had bent several of the bars. The door dangled from one hinge. As he watched, the forklift driver loaded the wreckage onto a flatbed truck.

With the cage's appearance, the nervous energy of the guards seemed to increase. One of them barked at two others to get the traffic moving and clear the area. Another approached Levi and his aggressor.

"What seems to be the trouble?" a second guard asked.

"This man is refusing to leave the area." The first guard gagged as he spoke. He wiped mucous from his cheeks and scowled.

The second guard nodded to Levi. "Your name, sir?"

"You don't need it," Levi said. "And I will not give it."

"Sir, when I ask you a question, you will answer me."

"I don't answer to you."

Before the men could respond, Levi flicked Dee's reigns

114

and guided the buggy back out into traffic, waving a brisk thanks to the Ford Explorer who signaled him permission to merge. Crowley relaxed again. Sighing, the dog turned in a circle and then lay down on the bench seat. As they clopped down the road, Levi glanced into the buggy's rearview mirror. The second guard had turned his attention elsewhere, but the one who Dee had sneezed on watched them leave, his expression incredulous and angry.

Levi scratched Crowley behind the ears with one hand and guided Dee with the other.

"Okay then," he said. "I suppose we'll just have to do this the hard way."

* * *

When they arrived back at home, Levi unhooked Dee and led her to the stable, where he spent a few extra minutes being extra attentive. He gave her a long brushing, and some fresh apples and carrots to go along with her regular feed. The horse snorted gratefully, tossing her head in delight. She crunched them slowly, with a thoughtful expression.

"Good girl," Levi said, kissing her muzzle. "That was well done."

He was overcome with a sudden surge of affection for the horse. Dee was descended from a long line, and her family had aided his for generations. He'd had her since she was a foal, and along with Crowley, she was probably his most loyal companion. It had never occurred to him before now just what would happen to Dee or Crowley were something bad to befall him. Who would care for them? Sterling? It was something he should make arrangements for. Others had life insurance to provide for their loved ones. He should do the same for his.

When it was completely dark, he once again gathered his belongings and his walking stick. Then, he whistled for Crowley, who was seemingly preoccupied with inhaling all of the food in his bowl with one giant gulp.

"Come on, boy. Let's go for a walk."

Crowley's ears perked up at this news. Tail wagging, he trotted over to Levi and panted happily. Levi quickly began to recite a prayer against all mishaps.

"I, Levi Stoltzfus, son of Amos Stoltzfus, will go on a journey tonight. I will walk upon God's way, and walk where God himself did walk, and our—"

A whippoorwill cried out from somewhere behind the barn, startling both Levi and the dog. It called again, its song echoing loudly in the darkness. Composing himself, Levi tried to remember where he'd left off. He faltered a few times before continuing.

"I am thine own, that no dog may bite me—"

Crowley whined.

"Quiet," Levi whispered. "This is for your protection, too, you know. Now, where was I? Oh, yes. No wolf may bite me, and no murderer may secretly approach me. Save me, oh my God, from sudden death. I am in God's hands and will thus bind myself by our Lord Jesus' five wounds, that any gun or other weapon may not do me any more harm than the virginity of our Holy Virgin Mary was injured by the favor of her beloved Jesus."

After this, he recited the Lord's Prayer and the articles of faith. Usually, this simple benediction gave him a sense of calm, assuredness, and strength—what Sterling's kids would have called getting "psyched" for the task ahead. But tonight, Levi felt none of those things. Frowning, he wondered why.

His thoughts turned again to Paimon.

"I'll find a way out of it. I'll find a way to make it right,

Lord. I just have to take care of this first."

Then, with Crowley running loose at his side, Levi headed into the woods toward Chickies Rock. Levi noticed that Crowley's tail had stopped wagging.

They slipped beneath the trees, following a crooked, winding path. It occurred to Levi that he'd been walking a similar path, in one incarnation or another, for most of his life.

FOUR

Parker knew he should be focused on the task at hand—tracking the creature and killing it with extreme prejudice before the public figured out just what an epic cluster-fuck had occurred. Instead, he found himself thinking about going hunting with his father. His old man had been gone four years now, after a mercifully short battle with cancer (the disease had already metastasized before he got his diagnosis). Parker had gotten used to his death, but there were still times when the longing and grief crept up on him, surprising him with how strong and powerful they still were. Thinking of their hunting trips always made him smile. He could still picture them clear as day—he and his father up at the crack of dawn, then heading out into the woods and fields for small game. They'd bagged countless rabbits, pheasants, and quail together. The two had never had much luck turkey hunting, but deer season had usually brought a buck for at least one of them.

Of course, those hunting trips were quite different than the one he was currently engaged in. Back then, he and his father had worn jeans, coats, and bright orange hunting vests. Now, Parker was decked out in camouflage, lightweight but sturdy body armor, combat boots, and a high-tech piece of headgear that supplied night-vision, infrared, communications, and even a GPS device. On trips with his father, he'd carried a 4-10 or a 30-06 that had once belonged to his uncle. Now, he was armed with a combat rifle so exclusive to Globe personnel that it didn't even have a commercial designation. Pictures of the weapon never popped up in gun magazines.

They weren't available for purchase at gun shows or stores. Civilians and even military personnel didn't know they existed. And, should he find himself in close quarters combat, he could switch over to the sidearm or knife strapped to his hips, both of which were also Globe exclusives.

Parker grinned, wondering what his father would think if he could see him now.

He was still grinning when something snuck up behind him and slashed through the back of his neck, talons expertly seeking a soft spot not covered by his body armor. Before he could scream, the creature reached into the wound and snapped his spine, just at the base of his brain.

Parker fell, thinking once more of his father.

* * *

For what must have been the fiftieth time since they'd disembarked from the plane at Harrisburg International Airport, Kinison silently cursed this entire mission. He'd had plans for tonight. Those plans had involved a redhead and her brunette friend, both of whom were known at the bar where he hung out as fans of men in uniform. It didn't matter who you were with—police, military, or a private security firm like Globe. If you carried a gun, chances were you could hook up with them for the night. Kinison had intended to do just that. What he hadn't planned on doing was hopping a flight to Pennsylvania Amish Country and sneaking around in the goddamned woods hunting for a fucking Bigfoot.

He manually switched the optics in his visor from thermo-graphics to normal. The night vision and infrared settings always gave him a headache, and given his current mood, a migraine wouldn't help the situation right now. Besides, it's not like the thing was showing up in any case. If it was giving off body heat, then it must have wings, because nothing was registering on the ground.

His ire turned to his superiors, and in turn, to their bosses, and then up the chain of command to the brain trust running the Globe Corporation itself. Whose idea had this been, anyway? Obviously, not anyone involved with the security division. Nobody in that department was that stupid. No, this shit sandwich had to have been cooked up by the dimwits in the media and entertainment division of the company. Those idiots were *always* fucking something up.

Kinison often thought that Globe's biggest problem was that it was simply too large. The corporation seemed to be involved with everything. Oil drilling, entertainment, fiber optics, medical technology, communications, medical research, publishing—you name it, chances were good that the Globe Corporation was making money from it. The public wasn't even aware of the entirety of the company's subsidiaries and interests. In truth, Kinison suspected that most of the shareholders weren't aware, either. But the security division was. Anytime there was a problem or a mess to be cleaned up, they were the ones tasked to deal with it.

Branches rustled in the treetops directly above him. Pausing, Kinison glanced upward in time to see a massive, dark form drop from the tree. The shape pummeled him to the ground, crushing Kinison beneath its weight. The beast knelt atop his chest, leering at him. Its liver-colored tongue protruded from between yellowish-white fangs, and snot dripped from its snout. The monster's stench was overwhelming—wet fur and animal musk. Kinison had time to utter a brief, weak gasp into his helmet microphone before his attacker's fingers closed around his throat. He felt claws digging into his skin as the creature seized his windpipe. Then, with a grunt, the beast ripped it out of his throat and tossed the organ aside.

Kinison's head followed a moment later.

* * *

Frowning, Linda stopped walking and listened. For a moment, she'd thought she heard something in her headset. They were under orders to maintain radio silence as much as possible, so there was no cross chatter or horseplay. She preferred it that way. As one of the few women assigned to this detachment, and the only one tapped for extermination and clean-up duty, she anticipated the usual comments and teasing from her male team members. That was standard operating procedure on missions past. Not all of them engaged in such behavior, of course. This was 2013, after all. But there were still a few men who hadn't gotten the memo that women were their equals, rather than their subordinates. A few of them, especially assholes like Kinison, were on the squad. Linda had expected him to have started in on her already, delivering crude innuendos over the headsets regardless of orders to remain silent, but so far, he'd behaved. She was especially grateful that he hadn't made any jokes about her being on the rag, when in fact, she was. She hated going out into the field when she was on her period. Although she knew it was paranoid, Linda often worried that her male team members would know it and would judge her for it.

When the sound wasn't repeated, she slowly started forward again, mindful of where she stepped, watching for fallen branches or piles of leaves that could alert the predator to her presence.

Simultaneously, she remained alert for their prey, watching the spaces between the trees and looking for stool or a stray tuft of fur snagged in passing by a vine or branch.

121

The forest was beautiful, and despite the present danger, Linda appreciated the serenity and foliage. But it was also eerily silent, and that unnerved her even more than Kinison's apparent good behavior.

Judging by the digital readout on the inside of her visor, she guessed that she was nearing the infamous precipice for which Chickies Rock got its name. The ground became more treacherous. Stones jutted from the dirt, forcing her to go around them time and time again. In the dark, the rugged landscape was a minefield of potential pitfalls, especially given the fact that she was simultaneously focused on finding their target and not getting killed in the process.

She frowned, catching a whiff of something nasty in the air, but before she could determine the source, a twig snapped behind her, sounding very loud in the darkness. Linda spun on her heels, knees locked, and her feet a shoulder's width apart, and brought her weapon up to fire. There was nothing behind her. The forest was empty.

She turned around to proceed and came face to face with the beast. She'd seen pictures of the creature and its kind before the briefing, but those pictures hadn't done justice to just how hideous and horrifying the things were up close. Its stench was terrible, even from three feet away. Its snout bore pale, ragged scars from some former battle, and its fur was covered with thorns, seed pods, and dirt. Flies buzzed around the monsters eyes and nose, but the thing barely seemed to notice them. Its attention was focused on her.

Fighting to remain calm, Linda clicked off the safety on her weapon. The beast's eyes darted downward, tracking the action, but it made no move to attack. Instead, its gaze met hers. Those black eyes seemed to study her almost longingly. Linda shuddered, remembering from the briefing how intelligent these animals were, and how, driven to the edge of extinction, they often attempted to mate with humans, gorillas, and similar mammals in a desperate effort to expand their line.

"This is Simmons," she said quietly into her microphone.

The creature stiffened, sniffing the air with its scarred snout.

"I've made contact," she reported, and edged her finger toward the trigger, not wanting to spook the beast.

The creature opened its broad mouth and grinned. It made a soft, purring noise in the back of its throat. With one hand, it reached down and groped itself between the legs.

Shit, she thought as her finger found the trigger. *This fucking thing is going to try to rape me.*

But it didn't. Instead, it lunged toward her, side-stepping the barrage that erupted from the barrel of her rifle, and slashed at her face with one clawed hand, ripping her cheek open and slicing through her helmet strap. Linda had time to scream before the claws of its other hand punctured her body armor and found the soft flesh of her abdomen beneath. Hissing, the beast knocked her weapon aside and clawed her face again, tearing her nose and lips to ribbons. Linda shrieked as her helmet slipped over her eyes.

Although she couldn't see what happened to her next, she felt it.

Luckily, it only lasted for a few brief seconds, and then she was silent again.

* * *

Ross, the team leader, whispered frantically into his headset as he rushed toward Linda's location.

"Filizzi, Kinison, Parker, Guthrie, Nazarek, James. Report."

"Copy, Ross," Filizzi said. "I've got Simmons on GPS. Proceeding to her location now."

"James and I approaching from the north," Guthrie replied. "No sign of it yet."

"Nazarek?" Ross asked. "What's your status?"

"Scared shitless," Nazarek replied. "I think we're going to need bigger guns."

"Stow that shit," Ross said. "Focus on the task at hand. Kinison and Parker, report?"

Neither man replied.

"Kinison? Parker?"

Ross regretted his decision to break protocol for this hunt. The squad should have been split up into four groups of two, but the team was anxious to get the job over with and get back home, and splitting up had allowed them to cover more ground quickly. Plus, he'd reasoned that it was only one creature, rather than a tribe. It was in unfamiliar territory and still half-drugged. How hard could it be to hunt the thing?

Pretty goddamned hard, as it turned out.

Ross pressed a button on his helmet and a GPS locator appeared on the inside of his visor. Multi-colored dots showed the location of each team member. Kinison, who was purple, and Parker, who was green, were both stationary, as was Simmons. The fact that none of them were moving, Kinison and Parker weren't responding, and Simmons had replied with screams and gunshots, followed by silence, did not bode well.

"Simmons..." Ross spoke quietly, but then decided to humanize his response a little more. "Linda. If you can hear me, but can't respond, just sit tight. We're coming in. You just hang on. Same goes for you, Parker and Kinison. Everyone else, converge on Simmons's location. Watch your asses. You were all briefed on this thing. A few of you were on the original island detachment. You all know what it's capable of. I'm guessing the tranquilizers are working their way out of its system faster than we were told to expect."

"Copy that," James said. "Guthrie and I are almost there."

"Affirmative," Guthrie confirmed. "No sign of it yet."

"I still think we should cancel this hunting trip and find the nearest bar," Nazarek replied. His voice lilted with barely-suppressed laughter.

Ross frowned. "Get your shit together, Nazarek. There's eight of us and one of it. We've got the advantage."

"Fuck me," Filizzi moaned over the headset.

"What's wrong?" Ross asked. "Do you have contact?"

"No," Filizzi said. "I hit a ravine. Wasn't on the map, and the GPS showed it as shallower than it really is. I'm gonna have to backtrack."

"We're almost there," James said. "Commencing radio silence."

* * *

The creature stood panting over the female's shredded form. It raised its claws to its mouth and licked the gore from them. Its muscles coiled, tense with frustration. Despite the fact that she'd been hunting him, the thing's natural biological urge had been to capture and mate with the woman, rather than kill her. But when she'd confronted it, and the beast had caught the scent of her menstruation and had known breeding would have not been successful, it had opted to kill her instead.

Memories surfaced, though somewhat distant and dull, made muted by the strange substance its captors had tricked it into ingesting—a substance which caused the creature to fall into a deep sleep. The thing remembered its tribe, and the trouble they'd had procreating. Generations of interbreeding on their island had resulted in hideous, obscene mutations, most of which were born sterile. The beast itself had a mutation, albeit less conspicuous than those of its kindred. It had been born with two sphincters, one of which was useless and had grown shut over time. Many in its tribe had been worse off, cursed with blindness, deafness, oversized appendages, missing or multiple limbs, functionless genitalia, albinism, and worse.

But then, others had arrived on the island. Hairless ones like those who had brought it here, to this new place. The tribe had sought to mate with the females of that other tribe, but instead, they'd been slaughtered. The few who had survived were placed into captivity. The beast had been among those prisoners until recently. Now, standing beneath the moon and the treetops, feeling the breeze ruffle through its fur and the soft loam of the forest floor beneath the thick pads of its feet, the creature vowed to not be captured again.

It finished licking the blood from its hands and fur. Then it paused, listening to the noise from elsewhere in the forest, as the rest of the hunters converged upon its position. To the beast, they sounded like a pack of boars lumbering through the woods. Despite their obvious caution, it heard every footfall, every word, and every breath. It smelled the gun oil on their weapons and the sour sweat from their pores. The creature still didn't understand why it had been brought to this place, but it understood all too well that these humans considered themselves the hunters and it the prey.

Grinning, the beast decided to change that.

As its pursuers drew near, the creature shimmied up a tree, directly over the female's lifeless form. Concealing itself in the branches, the beast waited.

126

* * *

As they hiked deeper into the forest, Levi's sense of foreboding deepened. He knew these woods as well as he knew his own backyard, and tonight, they felt *wrong*. Crowley sensed it, too. The dog continued tracking, and Levi had no doubt that the scent he followed was that of the creature they sought, but rather than running ahead or yipping excitedly like he normally did when on the hunt, Crowley stayed close by his side, venturing no more than a few feet ahead.

The feeling of dread worsened the farther they went. Levi was struck by the similarity between the county park's overall atmosphere tonight and the fearful atmosphere of LeHorn's Hollow. But while the latter, a place of myriad and perpetual evils, had always exuded that psychic warning, the woods around Chickies Rock had always been peaceful and serene, even at night. Albatwitch or no, before recent events, the worse thing that could befall a hiker here was a poisonous snake, a fall from the cliffs, a tumble down a ravine, or a rare chance encounter with a black bear.

Something else was here now, and the forest knew it. The wildlife, the plants, and even the ground itself were sending out warnings to any who knew the secrets of how to listen. And hear it, Levi did. He had no choice. He could no more turn off his psychic senses than he could other ones.

They started up a steep hill. Levi walked carefully, using his walking stick to support him as he wound his way around rocks and jutting tree roots. Crowley paused a moment, sniffing around to capture the scent again, and then started forward once more. Levi followed him.

Then the screams and gunshots started again.

FIVE

Levi didn't need Crowley's canine senses to smell the blood
ahead of them. He caught his first whiff before they had
even reached the top of the hill. Indeed, as the gunshots and
screams grew louder, Crowley's pace slowed considerably.
Clearly, the dog was hesitant to go any further, yet he was
also possessed of the desire to please his master. Levi
thought about sending him home again, but then decided that
Crowley would be safer at his side, at least for now.

The battle raged on ahead of them. The heavy arms fire
and unintelligible cries were punctuated by another noise—a
throaty, guttural growl. Then, as quickly as they had begun,
the sounds of fighting ceased, and the woods fell silent again.
Levi could have believed he hadn't heard any of it at all
were it not for the ringing in his ears, Crowley's reluctance
to proceed, and the stench borne on the wind. It reminded
Levi of when he was younger, and how his father's barn
had smelled after they'd butchered a hog or a steer. But as
they crested the top of the hill and paused, cautiously taking
cover behind a thicket of wild mulberry trees, Levi noticed
another smell, as well—something sour and animal. He was
certain it was an odor not native to Chickies Rock.

The moon came out from behind the clouds, lessening
the darkness. Levi crept out slowly from behind the bushes.
Crowley moved with him, pressed so tightly against his
leg that Levi almost tripped and fell. Both of them gaped
at the massacre before them. Bodies and pieces of bodies
were strewn about the hilltop. Tree trunks were splattered

with gore and innards dangled from branches. He counted seven corpses total, none of which was whole. Arms and legs had been torn from their sockets, necks and abdomens were torn open and emptied, and one unlucky individual's throat had been slashed with such severity that his head hung backward, attached to his body by only a thin flap of skin. Another victim sat with his back against a tree. A rifle had been thrust through his mouth and out the back of his head. Incredibly, the tip of the rifle barrel was embedded in the tree trunk. Levi marveled at the strength and ferocity it must have taken to accomplish such a thing. There were six men and one woman. Judging by the logo on their camouflage uniforms, all of them had worked for the Globe Corporation.

Crouched amidst the carnage, his boots covered in bloody mud, Levi was once more conflicted on whether to send Crowley home or not. The dog bent its head and sniffed a corpse. Then it looked up at him and whined.

"Go home," Levi whispered. "Go back to Dee and wait for me."

Crowley's ears perked up and he wagged his tail. He trotted over to his master, but then stopped. Cocking his head, he put his nose to the ground. Then, he snuffled toward a grouping of boulders several yards away. Levi glanced in that direction, heart pounding, expecting some horror to leap out from behind the rocks.

Instead, there was a very human moan of agony.

Rushing over to the boulders, Levi and Crowley found an injured Globe contractor lying on the ground. His right ear and part of his cheek were missing, and there were wounds on his arms, legs, and torso as well. His rifle lay discarded by his side. He looked up at them, blinking.

"I think I need a doctor," the man rasped.

"Then you're in luck." Levi crouched down next to the

injured man. "What is your name?"

"Nathan. Nathan Filizzi. Who are you? Am I...? Did it...? Shit! Where are the others?"

Ignoring the question, Levi whispered, "You're in shock. Is whoever did this to you still around?"

Filizzi nodded.

"Okay. I'm going to give you something to stop the bleeding and take away the pain. But we must be quiet. Do you understand?"

The injured man nodded again.

Using the thumb of his right hand, Levi made the sign of the cross three times over each of Filizzi's wounds. Then, still keeping his voice hushed, he said, "The word of God, the milk of Jesus' mother, and Christ's blood, is for all wounds and burnings good. Jesus Christ, dearest blood. That stops the pain and stops the blood."

He then began counting backwards from fifty, while Crowley stood watch. By the time he'd reached thirty, Filizzi had stopped squirming in pain and lay still. When Levi reached three, the bleeding had stopped. Though his wounds were still horrific to look at, the contractor's eyes and expression seemed clearer.

"How did you—?"

"It's an old family recipe." Levi smiled. "There were other options I could have chosen. Cutting three twigs from a tree and rubbing them in your wounds, for example, but this seemed the most expedient. Now, tell me what happened to you. What did this?"

"I don't know what its actual name is. We called it a cryptid."

"Who is 'we'?"

"My team. We were called in after it got loose. None of this was supposed to happen."

Levi glanced at Crowley, determining from the dog's behavior and posture that they were still in no immediate danger. Then he turned back to Filizzi.

"Perhaps you had better start at the beginning."

"It's classified, sir. I'm not supposed to talk about it."

Levi frowned. "I could make you talk. It would be very easy to start the bleeding again."

"You didn't let me finish. I said I wasn't supposed to talk about it. I didn't say I wouldn't. Truth is, with that thing still on the loose, we're both dead anyway. You'll never tell anyone because there's no way you or your dog are making it out of here alive tonight."

"The Lord shall be the judge of that," Levi said. "Now, please. Explain to me what has happened."

"You know much about the Globe Corporation?"

Levi shrugged. "I believe so, yes."

"Well, the entertainment division owns the network that produces *Cryptid Hunter*. The crew were in York County, filming an episode about a giant snake or something. Apparently, it didn't pan out, so some genius at the network decided they'd do something else instead. Apparently, they were filming just across the river, and they knew that over here on this side of the river, there were stories about miniature Bigfoots. Or is it Bigfeet?"

"You're talking about the legend of the Albatwitches?"

"I don't know what they were called. All I know is somebody at the network decided to stage the whole thing. You ever watch that show *Castaways*?"

"I am familiar with it, but I've never watched it."

"But I'm sure you heard about that incident a few years ago? Where most of the cast and crew died during a hurricane?"

Levi nodded.

131

"Well," Filizzi said, "that was all bullshit. The hurricane existed, but Globe covered up what really happened. See, they were filming *Castaways* on this supposedly deserted island. Except that it wasn't deserted. There were these monkey-things living there. Cryptids, they called them. Sort of like a Bigfoot, but way meaner. The tribe killed almost all of the cast and crew, and then the hurricane hit. Globe sent a team in to rescue the survivors and covered the whole thing up."

"And what of the creatures? What happened to them?"

"Supposedly, they were exterminated. But we found out later that the company kept some of them in captivity."

"How is any of this possible?"

"You see this thing for yourself," Filizzi said, "and you'll believe."

"Oh, not the creature," Levi replied. "I believe that full well. I'm just stunned that a single corporation could get away with something like this."

"Then you're not thinking big enough. Globe's name says it all. They're involved with everything—them, and maybe three or four other corporations just like them. These guys control the fucking world. Take the island, for example. They were able to hush it up because of their presence in the area. They owned the network producing Castaways, they owned the oil rig anchored off the coast, and they owned the security contractor sent in to mop up afterward. Anyone in government or law enforcement who knew about it, also knew enough to look the other way."

"But that still doesn't explain what's happening here?"

"Somebody at the network decided it would be a good idea to bring one of the cryptids from the island here, to your hometown. They kept it drugged on tranquilizers and caged. They were going to release it here, still in its drugged state, and then have the *Cryptid Hunter* team 'capture' it on camera. Guess they'd offer it as proof of your local legend. The whatever you called them."

"Albatwitches."

"Yeah, those. It would have been a ratings blockbuster. But the fucker wasn't as doped up as they thought because it busted loose from the cage and tore off into the woods. Slaughtered its handlers and that's when we got the call to come in and clean up the mess. It killed a local girl while we were en route. And now it's massacred my team."

His voice grew thick, and he choked off a sob. Shuddering, Filizzi reached for Levi and grasped his arm.

"Thanks for helping me," he whispered, "but you realize we're fucked, right? That thing's still out there. Sooner or later, it will come back."

"Then you should leave. My dog can guide you out of the forest and protect you."

"Like this?" Filizzi glanced down at his wounds. "I can't go five feet like this."

"You're gravely injured, yes. But the bleeding won't start again, and you've no broken bones. Just a few bruised ribs."

"How can you tell that?"

"I have my ways."

Filizzi studied him a moment. "You're crazy. Everyone's crazy. My bosses. You. The whole fucking world."

Whining, Crowley sniffed the air.

"Yes," Levi agreed, "your employers would certainly qualify as crazy. It seems to me it would have been much easier to simply fly the television crew to this island you mentioned, rather than transporting the beast here in a populated area. That speaks to a level of arrogance and indifference that certainly borders on insanity."

"You've got no idea. This is just the tip of the iceberg.

All that crazy conspiracy stuff you read about on the Internet? The New World Order and the Globalists and the Technocrats? I don't know if it's real or not, but if so, Globe would certainly fit right in. I hear all kinds of shit. People say that they're practicing eugenics. Population control. Destabilizing national currencies so they can introduce something different. Some people say the higher ups worship a cat. A guy I used to work with told me he heard they want to eventually replace humanity with machines. Probably a lot of it is nonsense, but still..."

Crowley lowered his head and growled.

"Easy, boy," Levi whispered. "What is the name of this cat they worship?"

Filizzi shrugged. "I don't know. He said it was spelled with a K. That's the only other part I remember. We were drinking at the time. Kat-with-a-K."

Levi was visibly startled, but before he could respond or press the injured man for more information, a bestial roar echoed through the forest.

Filizzi paled. "It's coming back."

Branches snapped and leaves rustled. Whatever was coming toward them sounded massive. The creature snarled again some-where in the darkness. Crowley hunkered down and bared his teeth, emitting an answering growl. Levi spotted two small saplings shaking violently as the beast plodded toward them. The monster's stench preceded it, strong enough that—despite his fear—Levi fanned his nose.

"Stay here," Levi whispered to Filizzi. "You're well-concealed behind these boulders. Crowley and I will lead it away."

Filizzi grabbed Levi's arm. "You can't—"

"There is no time to argue, I'm afraid." Levi gently but firmly disengaged from the injured man and then clambered over the boulders.

The animal's musk grew stronger. More trees trembled. The unseen creature snorted. The sound reminded Levi of an angered bull preparing to charge. He glanced down at Crowley.

"See? I told you that you should have gone home."

Crowley growled again in response, then grew silent as the creature emerged from the trees. It wasn't what Levi had expected. It stood barely five feet high, and its head seemed too small for its body. Likewise, its lower jaw seemed grossly larger than the rest of its face. Except for its face and genitalia, the beast was covered in curly brown hair. Its legs, arms, and chest bulged with powerful muscles, and Levi had no doubt it could crush him to death just by squeezing, should he be unfortunate enough to land in the monster's grasp. It also possessed long, curved claws on both its feet and hands that looked sharp enough to cut through wood. Perhaps the most hideous part of its physiology were its penis and testicles. Like its jaw, they seemed overlarge in comparison to the rest of the creature's body.

Despite its monstrous visage, Levi could sense nothing supernatural about the beast. Its aura was like that of any other living being, and there were no signs of inter-dimensional manifestation or summoning. Indeed, the creature looked remarkably similar to pictures he'd seen in various cryptozoological research books and websites—perhaps a shorter, distant cousin of the creatures in the infamous Crazy Bear Valley sighting or the long-lost kin of Florida's Skunk Ape. One thing was for certain—the thing standing before them was certainly not an Albatwitch.

"Are you intelligent?" Levi wondered aloud. "Can you understand me?"

The creature stopped growling and tilted its head, staring

at both man and dog with a puzzled expression. Its nostrils flared wide as it sniffed the air. Slowly, it flexed its fingers, clacking its talons together.

"We mean you no harm." Levi fought to keep the fear out of his voice, trying to project calmness. "You are a long way from home and against your will. I'd be angry too, were I in such a situation. Perhaps I can help you."

The creature bared its fangs and snarled. Then it took another step toward them. Crowley growled in response. Levi noticed blood on the beast's side. Apparently, it had been injured during its fight with Filizzi's teammates. He couldn't see the wound through the fur, but he assumed that it must not be too bad, judging by the cryptid's behavior.

"Hbbi Massa danit Lantien." Levi recited several charms, hoping to strengthen both Crowley and himself and give them an advantage over the aggressor. "Ut nemo in sense tentat, descendere nemo. At precedenti spectatur mantica tergo."

He'd barely finished when the beast lunged at them. Crowley sprang to meet the attack. The cryptid roared as the dog's jaws snapped shut on its thick forearm. Furious, the creature shook its arm, trying to dislodge Crowley, but to Levi's horror and admiration, the dog hung on tight, burrowing his teeth deeper into the thing's hide.

Levi swung at the creature's legs with his walking staff, but the monster stepped back out of range. The beast swung its arm again, smashing Crowley against a gnarled tree trunk. The dog yelped in pain and fell to the ground, writhing. Levi swung again, aiming this time for the creature's head. He cried out in dismay as the staff splintered, cracking in half and leaving him holding a shortened spear. The blow seemed to have no effect on his foe.

"That wasn't supposed to happen," Levi gasped.

His opponent made a noise that might have been laughter. Then it swiped at him with one long arm. Its talons raked across Levi's chest, ripping through his vest and the cover of his copy of *The Long Lost Friend*, which had been concealed in his pocket. Levi's fear turned to panic as the gouged book fell to the ground. He had a flash of memory—his battle with a supernatural foe in the town of Brinkley Springs, West Virginia. That enemy had attacked him in a similar manner, but when its claws had come in contact with the book, there had been a magical reaction, repelling his foe. That should have happened now, as well.

But it hadn't, and the fact that it hadn't was more terrifying to Levi than the beast itself.

His chest burned. He felt blood welling from the wound the cryptid had delivered—a wound which should not have been possible, because *The Long Lost Friend* was supposed to prevent such things from happening. The inscription inside the book assured it. The book was the most important item in Levi's arsenal, a tool for both offense and defense, and it had never failed him before now.

So stunned was Levi by the sudden turn of events that he didn't notice the creature preparing another attack. It swung at him with both arms this time, two potentially killing blows that would have slashed through both his face and abdomen. But a second before it struck, Crowley bit the cryptid's leg, throwing it off balance. Shrieking in surprise, the beast turned its attention on the dog. Levi shook off his shock and jabbed the broken end of his walking staff at the monster's stomach. At the same time, Crowley released its leg and darted between its knees, going for the thing's testicles. The monster reared back, scampering away from them both. Man and dog stood side by side again, panting.

"Lord," Levi prayed, "my faith in You remains steadfast.

I do not understand why—"

Grunting, the beast lowered its head and charged. Levi thrust at it with the spear, but the cryptid merely shrugged off the attack and delivered a backhanded blow that knocked the magus off his feet.

Crowley, seeing his master's peril, barked at the monster, garnering its attention. Then he turned tail and ran, enticing their opponent to pursue him with a series of yips and barks. The monster took the bait and charged off after the dog, knocking saplings aside and churning up the rocky soil with its clawed feet. Both disappeared into the darkness.

Levi struggled to stand. His legs were wobbly and the pain in his chest grew worse. He snatched up his copy of *The Long Lost Friend*, lamenting its damaged condition. The book had been handed down to him from his father, and was beyond mere sentimentality. Ostracized from his community as he was, it was one of the few links Levi still had to his family.

Somewhere on the distant highway, a tractor-trailer applied its airbrakes. The sound seemed surreal in the midst of the carnage. Out here in the dark, standing atop Chickies Rock and surrounded by forest and night, it was easy to forget that the towns of Columbia and Marietta were just a few miles away. Levi shuddered to think what would happen if the cryptid managed to reach either municipality.

"Mr. Filizzi?" He kept his voice low. "Are you okay?"

The Globe employee groaned in response.

"Stay here," Levi whispered. "I'll come back for you, if I'm able."

Levi plunged into the forest, following the wake of destruction left by the creature. He could hear both it and Crowley farther ahead of him, engaged in a deadly game of cat and mouse. He needed to end the pursuit before Crowley came to harm. Levi figured he had enough ghosts following him. He didn't want to add that of his dog.

He found them moments later at the edge of Chickies Rock itself. The area was surrounded by converging hiking trails and a wooden boardwalk. The paths were layered with gravel. The forestry service had installed wooden handrails ten feet back from the cliff's edge to keep visitors away, and had hung signs warning people to keep back. The safety rules didn't apply to dog and beast, however. Both had ventured beyond the safety rails, and were dangerously close to the edge of the precipice, circling each other warily. Canine and cryptid were at a stalemate. Each time the beast grabbed or lunged for Crowley the dog darted around it or between the monster's legs. Every time Crowley tried to bite it however, he had to scamper clear of its reach before his teeth could find purchase.

Levi felt an immense swelling of pride in the dog. The monster had effortlessly dispatched an entire squad of special operations personnel, but Crowley was giving it a challenge. But that would soon change if he didn't act now.

Levi's boots crunched on the gravel as he ran toward them. Crowley kept his attention focused on his foe, but the beast glanced at Levi. As the magus vaulted over the nearest handrail and clambered out onto the rocks, Crowley took advantage of his opponent's distraction and leapt for the creature's throat. The beast moved at that last instant, and instead of the soft part of its neck, Crowley's jaws snapped shut on its furry shoulder instead. Enraged, the cryptid howled in pain and seized the dog in both hands. It tugged on Crowley, but the dog bit harder, refusing to let go. The creature's efforts became fiercer—almost panicked. With a mighty yank, it tore the dog free and tossed him into a boulder. Crowley's howl was cut short by a sickening crunch. Then he lay still.

Anguished, Levi rushed toward his friend, but the beast darted forward to meet him, reaching the fallen dog seconds before Levi did. Before he could escape, the creature grabbed Levi with both hands and lifted him off the ground. The cryptid's claws dug in to Levi's hip and shoulder, drawing fresh blood. The beast hefted him over its misshapen head. Levi feared it was about to dash him on the rocks or break his back. Then, in horror, he realized it intended to do something even worse.

In five quick strides, the beast carried him to the edge of the cliff. Levi's stomach lurched as he caught a glimpse of the river and train tracks far below. Lights twinkled from a farmhouse on the York County side of the Susquehanna. Further north he spied the Accomac Inn. To the south, a few trucks raced across the Route 30 bridge, oblivious to his plight. Then the beast turned him, and all Levi saw were stars.

Grunting, the creature tossed him over the side.

Levi shrieked as he fell—a long, high-pitched wail that was cut short only when his pin-wheeling arms smacked against the side of the cliff. He scrabbled at the stones, desperately seeking purchase. The fingernail on his left index finger peeled backward. Screaming, Levi fell again. He slammed into a slim rock ledge fifteen feet below, and then slid further down to a haphazard outcropping of rocks and tree roots. The debris halted his fall, but the force of Levi's landing dislodged several smaller stones. He realized that it wouldn't support his weight, and was likely to give way at any moment, plunging him the rest of the way down to the train tracks far below. He idly wondered if the same thing had happened to the woman, April Nace, before her death.

Shock, he thought. *I must be going into shock.*

He tasted blood in his mouth, and spat bright red into the yawning space below. His vision blurred. When it cleared again, Levi heard movement above him. He looked up and was horrified to see his attacker beginning a descent. The thing was a natural climber, working its toes, fingers, and claws into tiny cracks and crevices in the rock face. It jumped from boulder to boulder, closing the distance between them. When it growled at him, its fangs flashed white in the moonlight.

Levi started to move, but more of his perch gave way and tumbled off into the darkness. He heard rocks and bits of wood smashing far below, and stopped moving, opting instead to hug the cliff face and pray.

"Lord, I am sorry for whatever I have done to offend You. I know that I sometimes departed from your ways, and used the methods of the enemy instead, but even then, it was to serve Your glory, and defend Your creation. I ask now only that—"

Levi paused. His eyes grew wide as inspiration hit him. Of course! Just because *The Long Lost Friend* and his powwow disciplines had failed him didn't mean that he was defenseless. If those ways didn't work, he was just as adept in other forms and schools of magick.

As the creature drew nearer, close enough that he could smell its stench, Levi thought back to the 16th century alchemical works of Paracelsus, an early practitioner of both elementalism and geomancy. The latter would not help him now, but the former allowed the magus to control the elements—earth, water, fire, and air.

The cryptid crept closer. Ignoring it, Levi closed his eyes and tried to remember the correct process. It had been a long time since he'd practiced elemental magick, and a mistake now would cost him everything. There would be no time for second chances. He closed his eyes and slipped into an immediate trance—an ability he'd developed through years of necessity. He visualized the particular boulder that the creature was currently clinging to. Then Levi imagined himself behind the boulder, embedded within the cliff itself. He took seven deep breaths, and with each one, he pictured himself breathing in the rocks and soil. On the seventh breath, Levi held it, and then exhaled with force. His eyes snapped open as the cliff-face shook. There was a great roaring sound from deep within the earth and then, before the beast could react, the boulder it was clinging to was pushed from the mountainside by the earth itself. Soil and loose rocks poured from the hole like rushing water, sending the boulder and its unwitting passenger tumbling below. Dirt continued to blast from the hole. The cliff trembled a few more times. Then Levi sighed and the shaking stopped.

He risked a peek over the side of his perch and saw the boulder laying on the railroad tracks. The cryptid's legs stuck out from beneath it. A spreading pool of blood reflected the moonlight.

When Levi tried to crawl back up the cliff, his ledge shook, dislodging more debris. Worse, the pain made his vision blur again. There was a rushing sound in his ears. Levi tilted his head, willing himself not to pass out. His body refused to obey.

The last thing he remembered before he passed out was the sound of a whip cracking.

* * *

When he regained consciousness, the first thing Levi was aware of was that something was licking his face. He recognized the slobbery tongue and worried whimpers behind it even before he opened his eyes.

"Crowley!"

The dog yipped happily.

Groaning, Levi sat up slowly and checked himself over. None of his limbs seemed broken, but his mouth was sore and he still tasted blood. He prodded around with his tongue, experimenting, until he found the source. He'd broken a tooth in the fall, and also bitten the inside of his cheek. The cuts in his chest, shoulder, and hip still hurt, but the bleeding seemed to have stopped.

Satisfied that he'd live, Levi pulled Crowley to him and checked the dog over. Crowley, too, would survive, but had suffered at least one bruised or cracked rib, and there was an ugly gash over his left eye.

"You're a good dog. Good dog."

Crowley thumped his tail in agreement.

Wincing, Levi tottered to his feet. He found a stick in which to help support himself and then glanced around in confusion, wondering what provenance had delivered him from the side of the cliff to here in the forest, just beyond the safety rails. The last thing he remembered was the creature falling to its death, and then the sound of...

The sound of a whip cracking.

The same sound that legend said accompanied sightings of the Albatwitches.

Squinting, Levi studied the ground. After a moment's search, he found what he was looking for. There in the moonlight were several set of footprints. The large ones belonged to the cryptid. Alongside them were those of Crowley and himself. Another set indicated the booted feet of one of the Globe personnel, perhaps having passed through this area before their attack. But a fifth set of tracks belonged to something different than any of those. They were similar to the cryptid's footprints, but smaller, and without the talons.

After carefully considering them for several minutes, Levi determined that the tracks had been made by more than one creature. Three or four, in fact. It was harder to tell where the footprints ended. They seemed to stop at the bases of the trees.

Levi glanced up into the branches, but the treetops were concealed in darkness.

"Thank you," he called. "And I'll tell no one of your existence here."

Crowley barked.

Levi's brow furrowed, troubled, as something else occurred to him. His powwow had only worked when he used it to aid Filizzi, but not when he'd needed it for himself. Something similar had happened during his attempted exorcism of Abalam. What did that mean? Could he only use his specific discipline to aid others, but not himself? Were his primary means of both offense and defense now gone? Had the Lord deserted him, and if so, what would happen next? His feeling of foreboding deepened.

Crowley barked again, rousing Levi from his thoughts.

"Okay," he muttered, grunting in pain as they began the slow trek back to Filizzi's hiding spot. "We'll help Mr. Filizzi, and then we'll go home. You can sleep in the house tonight. You certainly earned it. Good dog."

Crowley wagged his tail again in agreement. Levi's smile faded when he saw how pronounced the dog's limp was.

"Rest and recuperation for us both," Levi said. "And then, when we are better, I'm off to Columbus."

Crowley whined.

"No," Levi told him. "I am afraid neither you nor Dee will be accompanying me this time. You've had enough excitement for one year. And I'm fairly certain dogs are not allowed inside the world headquarters of the Globe Corporation."

Crowley cocked an ear and stared at him.

"Even though I walk through the valley of the shadow of death," Levi recited the fourth verse of the twenty-third Psalm, "I will fear no evil, for You are with me, Lord."

But as they followed the crooked path, Levi wondered if that was true anymore.

BRIAN KEENE is the author of over forty books, including *Darkness on the Edge of Town, Take The Long Way Home, Urban Gothic, Castaways, Kill Whitey, Dark Hollow, Dead Sea,* and *The Rising* trilogy. He's also written comic books such as *The Last Zombie, Doom Patrol* and *Dead of Night: Devil Slayer.* His work has been translated into German, Spanish, Polish, Italian, French and Taiwanese. Several of his novels and stories have been developed for film, including *Ghoul* and *The Ties That Bind.* In addition to writing, Keene also oversees Maelstrom, his own small press publishing imprint specializing in collectible limited editions, via Thunderstorm Books. Keene's work has been praised in such diverse places as *The New York Times*, The History Channel, The Howard Stern Show, CNN.com, *Publisher's Weekly,* Media Bistro, *Fangoria Magazine*, and *Rue Morgue Magazine.* Keene lives in Pennsylvania. You can communicate with him online at www.briankeene. com, on Facebook at www.facebook.com/pages/Brian-Keene/189077221397or on Twitter at @BrianKeene

deadite press

"Earthworm Gods" Brian Keene - One day, it starts raining-and never stops. Global super-storms decimate the planet, eradicating most of mankind. Pockets of survivors gather on mountaintops, watching as the waters climb higher and higher. But as the tides rise, something else is rising, too. Now, in the midst of an ecological nightmare, the remnants of humanity face a new menace, in a battle that stretches from the rooftops of submerged cities to the mountaintop islands jutting from the sea. The old gods are dead. Now is the time of the Earthworm Gods...

"Earworm Gods: Selected Scenes from the End of the World" Brian Keene - a collection of short stories set in the world of Earthworm Gods and Earthworm Gods II: Deluge. From the first drop of rain to humanity's last waterlogged stand, these tales chronicle the fall of man against a horrifying, unstoppable evil. And as the waters rise over the United States, the United Kingdom, Australia, New Zealand, and elsewhere-brand new monsters surface-along with some familiar old favorites, to wreak havoc on an already devastated mankind..

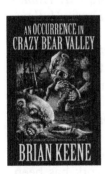

"An Occurrence in Crazy Bear Valley" Brian Keene- The Old West has never been weirder or wilder than it has in the hands of master horror writer Brian Keene. Morgan and his gang are on the run--from their pasts and from the posse riding hot on their heels, intent on seeing them hang. But when they take refuge in Crazy Bear Valley, their flight becomes a siege as they find themselves battling a legendary race of monstrous, bloodthirsty beings. Now, Morgan and his gang aren't worried about hanging. They just want to live to see the dawn.

"Entombed II" Brian Keene- It has been several months since the disease known as Hamelin's Revenge decimated the world. Civilization has collapsed and the dead far outnumber the living. The survivors seek refuge from the roaming zombie hordes, but one-by-one, those shelters are falling. Twenty-five survivors barricade themselves inside a former military bunker buried deep beneath a luxury hotel. They are safe from the zombies...but are they safe from one another?

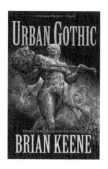

"Urban Gothic" Brian Keene - When their car broke down in a dangerous inner-city neighborhood, Kerri and her friends thought they would find shelter inside an old, dark row home. They thought they would be safe there until help arrived. They were wrong. The residents who live down in the cellar and the tunnels beneath the city are far more dangerous than the streets outside, and they have a very special way of dealing with trespassers. Trapped in a world of darkness, populated by obscene abominations, they will have to fight back if they ever want to see the sun again.

"Ghoul" Brian Keene - There is something in the local cemetery that comes out at night. Something that is unearthing corpses and killing people. It's the summer of 1984 and Timmy and his friends are looking forward to no school, comic books, and adventure. But instead they will be fighting for their lives. The ghoul has smelled their blood and it is after them. But that's not the only monster they will face this summer . . . From award-winning horror master Brian Keene comes a novel of monsters, murder, and the loss of innocence.

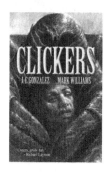

"Clickers" J. F. Gonzalez and Mark Williams- They are the Clickers, giant venomous blood-thirsty crabs from the depths of the sea. The only warning to their rampage of dismemberment and death is the terrible clicking of their claws. But these monsters aren't merely here to ravage and pillage. They are being driven onto land by fear. Something is hunting the Clickers. Something ancient and without mercy. *Clickers* is J. F. Gonzalez and Mark Williams' gore-soaked cult classic tribute to the giant monster B-movies of yesteryear.

"Clickers II" J. F. Gonzalez and Brian Keene- Thousands of Clickers swarm across the entire nation and march inland, slaughtering anyone and anything they come across. But this time the Clickers aren't blindly rushing onto land - they are being led by an intelligence older than civilization itself. A force that wants to take dry land away from the mammals. Those left alive soon realize that they must do everything and anything they can to protect humanity – no matter the cost. *This isn't war, this is extermination.*

AVAILABLE FROM AMAZON.COM

deadite
press

"Header" Edward Lee - In the dark backwoods, where law enforcement doesn't dare tread, there exists a special type of revenge. Something so awful that it is only whispered about. Something so terrible that few believe it is real. Stewart Cummings is a government agent whose life is going to Hell. His wife is ill and to pay for her medication he turns to bootlegging. But things will get much worse when bodies begin showing up in his sleepy small town. Victims of an act known only as "a Header."

"Red Sky" Nate Southard - When a bank job goes horrifically wrong, career criminal Danny Black leads his crew from El Paso into the deserts of New Mexico in a desperate bid for escape. Danny soon finds himself with no choice but to hole up in an abandoned factory, the former home of Red Sky Manufacturing. Danny and his crew aren't the only living things in Red Sky, though. Something waits in the abandoned factory's shadows, something horrible and violent. Something hungry. And when the sun drops, it will feast.

"Zombies and Shit" Carlton Mellick III - Twenty people wake to find themselves in a boarded-up building in the middle of the zombie wasteland. They soon discover they have been chosen as contestants on a popular reality show called Zombie Survival. Each contestant is given a backpack of supplies and a unique weapon. Their goal: be the first to make it through the zombie-plagued city to the pick-up zone alive. But because there's only one seat available on the helicopter, the contestants not only have to fight against the hordes of the living dead, they must also fight each other.

"All You Can Eat" Shane McKenzie - Deep in Texas there is a Chinese restaurant that harbors a secret. Its food is delicious and the secret ingredient ensures that once you have one bite you'll never be able to stop. But when the food runs out and the customers turn to cannibalism, the kitchen staff must take up arms against these obese people-eaters or else be next on the menu!

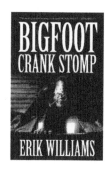
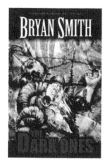
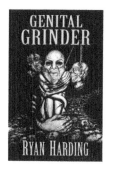

CPSIA information can be obtained at www.ICGtesting.com
Printed in the USA
LVOW04s1303260914

405825LV00006B/187/P